"I wanted you ... sexy outfits," C...

"No," responded Gabe vehemently. Seeing her in plain white bra and matching panties was viciously sexy enough, thanks very much!

She laughed and ignored his protest. When she had finished modeling her creations his heart was beating as if she'd run a marathon. Finally she slipped back into her jeans and shirt. "So? What did you think?" she asked eagerly.

What did he think? He thought he'd shaved ten years off his life with that sensual torture! "I thought it was very…nice."

"Nice?" She frowned at him. "I'm looking for devastatingly sexy. Come on, Gabe, work with me."

"Fine," he said, sighing deeply. "You were incredible. Satisfied?"

"Now that's what I wanted to hear!"

Dear Reader

I love fairy tales, but my sense of humour won't let me leave them alone. For example, what if Cinderella didn't *want* to change? What if she decided to go to the ball just to get a pushy fairy godmother off her back?

Enter my Cinderella-tomboy Charlotte Taylor. On the one hand she's got two relentless 'fairy godmothers', determined to get her married no matter what she wants. On the other she's got her best friend, Gabe Donofrio, who will do anything to make sure she stays 'one of the guys'! Throw in a thousand-dollar bet, some makeover madness and an irresistible attraction between two best friends, and you get *The Cinderella Solution*.

I hope you enjoy reading this as much as I enjoyed writing it. Drop me a line at PO Box 1239, San Leandro, CA 94577, USA, and let me know what you think.

Cathy Yardley

THE CINDERELLA SOLUTION

BY
CATHY YARDLEY

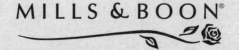

MILLS & BOON®

To my friends and family for supporting my insanity.
And to my critique group: Alyssa Ganezar, Ruth Barges,
Rose Murray, John Lovelady and Christina Crooks.
Thanks for believing in me.

First published in Great Britain 2002
Harlequin Mills & Boon Limited,
Eton House, 18-24 Paradise Road, Richmond, Surrey TW9 1SR

© Cathy Yardley 2000

ISBN 0 263 82943 X

Set in Times Roman 10½ on 11¼ pt.
01-0602-49932

Printed and bound in Spain
by Litografia Rosés, S.A., Barcelona

1

"I'M GOING TO KILL HIM," Charlotte muttered, hitting the accelerator on her car awkwardly in her satin high heels. "I'm going to get through this wedding without throwing up, and then I'm going to kill him."

The tires squealed as she tore into St. Mary's lot, cutting the curve just a little too close. She whimpered. Her morning-after headache punched at her brain like a prizefighter.

Of all the days to be hungover, this was the red-letter worst.

Her car screeched to a stop and she yanked up the emergency brake. She took a quick glance in the rear-view mirror, grimacing at the pale greenish cast to her face. "I'm going to kill him," she repeated.

She groaned as she wriggled out of her car, no small feat in her constricting pale-pink bridesmaid dress. She slammed the door shut, then gagged as the sound rang through her head. She rarely drank and had only experienced a hangover once before. She didn't remember how bad that had been, but it couldn't have been as bad as this. *Nothing* could be as bad as this.

"There you are, Charlie," a male voice boomed from the front steps. "We've been waiting for you!"

She was wrong. There *was* something worse. "I am going to kill you," she whispered.

Gabe Donofrio smiled mischievously at her from

the top of the stairs. He looked handsome, as usual, she noted with disgust. That gorgeous summer tan he kept all year long held no tinge of post-party green. His gray eyes weren't bloodshot, but lit with devilish humor. His dark hair and bright smile made him look as if he ought to be on the cover of a magazine. He looked as if he'd passed the previous evening curled up with a book and a glass of warm milk, when she knew perfectly well how he'd spent his night. He'd spent it making sure she'd be miserable this morning!

"Well, well, well." Gabe eyed her curiously, meeting her halfway down the stairs but wisely staying out of arm's reach. "Feeling a trifle ill this morning, are we?"

"Shut up. This is all your fault." She gripped the cold steel banister as if it were a life preserver, while her stomach did a queasy little dance step. "What in the world possessed you to con me into crashing Brad's bachelor party, anyway?"

"What were your options? If you'd stayed at my mom's house with my sister the bride, and her sidekick, Dana, you'd have gone crazy. Now that Bella's getting married, you're the last one." Gabe laughed. "You realize, of course, that now they're not going to rest until you're hitched."

She wished he were lying. The headache exploded dully behind her eyes, and her stomach constricted. "So you thought, say, the best way to prepare Charlotte for the grilling she's going to get tomorrow is…I know! Having her watch a half-naked exotic dancer freeze her butt off on a beach!"

"Actually, I just figured I'd pour ten tequila poppers down you, and at least cheer you up for a few hours," he said with a grin. "Come on, Charlie. Nobody held a gun to your head and made you drink."

"You bet me!" She poked a finger at him. "You

bet me a month's worth of car washes that I couldn't keep up with you. In the name of female honor, I had to pop that inflated ego of yours."

"Female honor? Oh, right, that's it," he said, laughing. "You've been this way since we were eight. You can't turn down a wager with me to save your life."

"Wanna bet?" She glanced over her shoulder at him, then stuck her tongue out.

"And, I might add—" his quicksilver eyes twinkled with amusement "—I've been beating you since you were eight."

"Shut *up.*" She eyed him balefully. "Or I'll throw up on your Armani suit."

"And wouldn't that go gorgeously with the decor," he quipped, glancing into the church. "I think Bella's got every gardenia in Southern California crammed in there. Honestly, I don't know how someone as girly as my sister wound up with a nice, normal friend like you."

Charlotte stepped into the small foyer of the church and stopped dead, assaulted by the overpowering floral scent. In her hungover state, the smell almost knocked her off of her feet.

"Oh, no." She started taking quick, shallow breaths. "Oh, God."

"Huh? Oh, *nuts.* Hold on, angel." Gabe was at her side in a flash, the teasing look replaced with one of serious concern. He anchored her with one strong arm. "Take it easy, you're going to be fine. They can wait a few more minutes," he assured her, his voice low and comforting.

Charlotte fought the urge to sit down on the step and ride out her wave of nausea, knowing that if she sat down, she'd never get back up. "How does Bella look?'' she asked, more to get her mind off her stomach than anything.

Gabe shrugged. ''Like she was caught in a lace factory that exploded.''

Charlotte chuckled appreciatively. Slowly, the pounding in her head and the churning in her stomach receded. ''If her dress is half as uncomfortable as this one, I pity her.''

''She's getting married. I pity her already,'' Gabe said, but his face still showed concern. ''Feel better?''

''Not tremendously,'' Charlotte said, sighing, ''but it'll have to do. My only goals for today are not throwing up on anyone, and avoiding the killer question.''

He snickered. ''You mean,'' he said, mimicking a nasal feminine whine, '''So, when are *you* getting married, Charlotte?'''

''Exactly.'' Charlotte tried to ignore the pang the question caused, even asked as a joke. It seemed as if she'd been facing questions like that forever.

When are you going to find a nice boy, Charlotte?

Why can't you be more like the other girls, Charlotte?

How do you expect to catch a man looking like that, *Charlotte?*

She was single by choice, she reminded herself. She'd said the words so often, she ought to have them tattooed on her forehead.

''You know, you wouldn't keep getting hit with these questions if you'd stop saying yes to being a bridesmaid. What is this? Three times?''

''Four,'' she corrected him, pulling herself stiffly upright.

''Oh, right. After four tours of duty as a bridesmaid, you know my family is going to hassle you into becoming a bride yourself. Besides, I know you.

You're not exactly the type who swoons over china patterns and floral arrangements. Why not sit one out?''

''It's *Bella,* Gabe,'' she said crossly. ''I probably should have turned down the earlier weddings, but Dana and your sister… I had to say yes. They're like my family.'' She lurched up to the foyer of the church. ''Your family has actually *been* my family since Dad passed away.''

''I know,'' Gabe said, subdued, then he chuckled. ''I think I figured that out when my mother asked when *you* were going to give her a grandchild.''

Charlotte felt it again, that little pang, but it was different this time. It wasn't just frustration, she noticed. It was suspiciously like envy. ''The point is, I'd do anything for my friends, Gabe. You know that. The only reason I haven't murdered *you* is the fact that you're my best friend.'' She smiled at him weakly. ''But I swear, if you pull another stunt like last night's bet, I won't be responsible for my actions. Got it?''

''Of course, of course. I wouldn't dream of it.'' Gabe nodded solemnly, but a smile still haunted the corners of his lips.

When they stepped into the church, she saw ten pairs of eyes snap toward them eagerly. All of Gabe's aunts homed in on her, calculating smiles on their faces.

''So I guess you won't bet me a month's worth of laundry that you can successfully avoid my aunts at the reception?'' Gabe whispered gleefully. ''Before you got here, I sort of suggested that you might be interested in their advice in the man-hunting department.''

''Make it two months,'' Charlotte said through gritted teeth, "and remind me to kill you when this is all over."

"I'M LOOKING FOR CHARLOTTE," Gabe yelled over the din of the speakers and the laughing, boisterous couples on the dance floor. "She disappeared on me right after we took pictures. Have you seen her?"

"Nah, I haven't," his friend Sean replied, looking at the crowd of guys near him for a response. They all shook their heads. "If you see her, though, tell her we're having a poker match tonight at Mike's."

Gabe nodded. "If anything would get her out of hiding, it's a good game of poker. Thanks."

He continued his slow tour of the large ballroom. He was so intent on tweaking Charlotte out of her gloom and giving her something to do at this reception other than focus on the "killer question," that he'd forgotten he was the target of that same question himself…and not from his aunts. He'd been circling the reception hall for more than an hour, looking for Charlotte, while trying to avoid being singled out. Emphasis on "single."

Ordinarily, he wouldn't mind a room filled to the rafters with pretty single women. But this was a wedding, and that changed the rules. Suddenly, asking a woman to dance was tantamount to handing her a ring. It was a dedicated bachelor's nightmare, Gabe reflected. If he had Charlotte by his side, at least he'd have a better chance at fending off the hungry stares and blatant invitations. It figured that the girl he was searching for was the one girl in this whole sea of single women who wasn't looking for matrimony in general, or him in particular!

He sighed. She might say she was ready to kill him, but that wasn't what was keeping her hidden. He sensed that there was more to Charlotte's avoidance than just being frustrated with his family's gentle pressuring, or their inability to accept her tomboy ways. It went deeper than that. Whatever it was, it tripped warning lights in his head. For all their pranks and high jinks, the bottom line was, she was his best friend on earth. If she avoided him for this long, she wasn't angry, she was upset. And he was going to find out why if he had to drag it out of her...or bet it out of her.

He felt a hand on his shoulder and tensed.

"There you are, bro'."

Gabe turned, grinning his relief. "Hey, Brad. So, how does it feel being married to my sister?"

Brad smiled, his light brown eyes lighting up like candles. "I've never been happier in my life."

"So you say now," Gabe joked, giving his new brother-in-law a friendly punch on the arm.

"Trust me," Brad said, "when you find the right girl, there is nothing in the world that feels more perfect. Nothing at all."

"I'll take your word for it." Gabe shifted his weight uncomfortably. "It seems like I'm surrounded by women who would like to be *anybody's* 'right girl.' Weddings seem to cause some weird chemical imbalance in women. If I asked any one of the single women here if they'd run off to Vegas to get married tonight, I think they'd do it in a heartbeat." He gazed around the room, shaking his head. "And they don't even know me!"

"Which is the only way they'd agree to it," Gabe heard Charlotte mutter darkly behind him.

He spun around. "There you are..."

But she wasn't. He caught a glimpse of her weaving away from him, disappearing into the party guests. Before he could follow, Brad spoke up.

"Was that Charlotte?" Brad craned his neck to

squint at her disappearing form. "You know, this morning when I saw her walking up the aisle, I barely recognized her. It was probably all those curls…and I don't remember the last time I saw her in a dress."

"The hangover didn't help," Gabe added, trying in vain to track her. "I dragged her to the bachelor party last night and bet her she couldn't drink as much as I could."

Brad scowled. "You brought a woman to my bachelor party?"

"No, I brought Charlotte. There's a difference." When Brad didn't look mollified, Gabe shrugged. "I kept her off in the corner, Brad. Besides, she's been one of the gang for years, and we didn't do anything even remotely shocking."

"It's the principle of the thing, Gabe. You know, No Girls Allowed?" Brad shook his head, finally laughing a little. "And Charlotte's not a bad-looking girl, either, when she gives it a shot. I can only imagine what she looks like when she's not green. Of course, it might help if she didn't look like she was plotting your murder, either."

"She'll get over it. It might take a while, but she always does. Hell, half the time her practical jokes are worse than mine." Gabe laughed. "Did I tell you what she did last week—"

"Hi, Gabe."

The two men turned to see a lush-lipped blonde, staring at Gabe with deep blue eyes. Her voice was husky, but slightly overdone.

"I've been watching you run around all night, Gabe. You're missing out on a great party. Want to dance?"

Gabe sighed. "Sorry, I'm looking for someone right now. Maybe later." Like in twenty years.

"You sure?" she drawled, making a seductive little

shimmy that did nice things to her dress. "Whoever you're looking for could probably wait a little while."

Gabe sighed even harder. *Charlotte, where the heck are you?* "Really, I'm sorry."

The woman pouted. "Suit yourself."

"Whoa." Brad watched her shimmy back into the crowd, then turned to Gabe. "You're out of your mind! How could you turn down an opportunity like that?"

"She had 'husband-hunter' written all over her, and I don't play that anymore." Gabe shuddered. "No, thanks."

"Aw, come on. It was one dance. You could find Charlotte later...."

"Let me explain something," Gabe said seriously. "When I was younger, I had a few serious relationships. One even came close to marriage. All of them ended like train wrecks."

"Ouch." Brad shook his head. "But what does that—"

"My friends were the only thing that got me through them," Gabe said seriously. "That's when I figured it out. I don't do commitments anymore. Why should I? I party with the guys whenever I want, I have a job most men would kill for, and I have a best friend who knows me inside and out, who's there for me twenty-four, seven. Women come and go...."

"With a rather high turnover rate, in your case," Brad interjected.

"But friends are forever." Gabe smiled smugly. "If I just stick to that, I have, literally, the perfect life."

Brad laughed. "I've got to admit, it sounds attractive. But there's just one problem."

"At the moment, it's Charlotte," Gabe conceded.

"But she never stays mad at me for long. She'll feel better as soon as she gets even."

"The problem is," Brad continued, "you're going to fall in love one of these days. And that's going to throw your perfect life for a loop."

"Never happen." Gabe winked. He'd caught sight of Charlotte, speaking with some young women over by the side of the dance floor. "I've got it all under control."

Before he could make a move toward Charlotte, the women swarmed over to where he and Brad were standing.

"Oh, I think it's wonderful," one of the women gushed.

He blinked at her. "What is?"

"That you want so desperately to adopt a young child to love, you're going to ask someone to marry you tonight!"

Surrounded by beaming, hopeful faces, he looked over to the other side of the room to see Charlotte grinning at him from ear to ear.

"Yup," Brad said, patting him on the shoulder. "Obviously. You've got it all under control."

CHARLOTTE WOULD HAVE BEEN enjoying her revenge on Gabe a lot more if his sister and Dana hadn't finally cornered her. Reluctantly, she went up to the hotel room the Donofrios had rented, flanked by the two girls, as if she were a prisoner. While she had managed to avoid the aunts, these two could not be dodged.

"I'm telling you, Charlotte," Bella wheedled, "this book will solve all your problems."

"Why are you punishing me?" Charlotte groaned, throwing herself on the king-size bed. "I got here, even though I was green as spinach and my head was ready to explode. I even wore pink, for pity's sake! What do you want now? My blood?''

"We just want to see you happy…and we want you to read one little book,'' Bella said, calmly taking off her wedding veil. She grabbed her dark-rose traveling suit off a low chair in the corner. "Don't let her get away, Dana,'' Bella instructed, her eyes glinting mischievously as she held up a wispy little nothing of white lace. "I have to get into Brad's surprise gift.''

"No problem,'' Dana said, her eyes never leaving Charlotte.

Charlotte sighed. There was no escape.

Dana tossed the slim paperback on the bed. Picking it up, Charlotte read the cover out loud. *"The Guide… How to Go from Miss Wrong to Mrs. Right in One Year.''* She groaned again, pushing her face into a pillow. "You have *got* to be kidding me.''

"It worked for me,'' Dana said, tugging Charlotte into a sitting position. "And it worked for Bella. You can't argue with success. Bella's practically glowing. Don't you want to be as happy as she is?''

"Bella got the last good man on earth,'' Charlotte muttered, eyeing the pillow. She would have made another dive for it, but for all of Dana's petite, sophisticated looks, the woman had the grip of a wrestler. "Why is it when your friends get married, they suddenly expect you to?''

"You're twenty-eight, Charlotte,'' Dana said firmly. "Hear that ticking? That's your biological clock.''

"I'm hitting the snooze button.''

"Denial,'' Dana announced, grabbing Charlotte's chin and angling her face until they were eye to eye. "You've been out of the dating scene for too long. Ever since you graduated from college, you've been burying yourself in that design firm and hanging out with those guys…what do they call themselves?''

"The Hoodlums," Charlotte said.

"Right. I don't know how many sets of baggy jeans and grubby sweatshirts I've seen you go through."

"Everybody wears casual clothes at work," Charlotte argued. "I'd look stupid in anything else!"

Dana rolled her eyes. "You can dress casually and still dress like a female, Charlotte. As much as you complain about it, you look good in a dress. And your hair looks cute curled."

"Dana, you know I can't curl my own hair to save my life." She gestured to the ringlets that were now sticking haphazardly around her head. "I look like I've been electrocuted."

Dana huffed. "It's not that bad, and you know it. What's really bothering you?"

Charlotte just sat there for a minute, silent. There *was* something bothering her. It had all started when she got to the church and Gabe had reminded her: four tours of duty as a bridesmaid.

Always the bridesmaid.

She glanced at the book. *Miss Wrong…*

As much as she touted that she was "single by choice," the truth stared her in the face whenever she looked at her friends. Beside Dana and Bella, Charlotte had always felt like a dull brown wren standing next to exotic birds. They were beautiful and sophisticated. What's more, their beauty was complemented by flirtatious, sparkling personalities. No, Charlotte Taylor was about as sparkling and mysterious as a glass of milk.

She didn't want their arguments, or worse, their pity. So she couldn't tell them all that. She wouldn't.

"I just don't see what the big deal is," Charlotte

finally answered. "I know I've only had one serious relationship, but it was a really convincing experience, believe me. Now I'm enjoying my life. I've got a great job and great friends. Please, couldn't you just let it go?"

Before Dana could respond, Gabe popped his head through the doorway. "Hey! The car's revving, and so's the bridegroom," he yelled. "Where's Bella?"

"Getting her traveling suit on," Dana answered, obviously irritated with the interruption.

"Good grief," Gabe said, walking in and rolling his eyes. "What is it about women that takes them so long to get dressed? It's never taken me that long to get clothes *off* of a woman."

"And Lord knows, you've had practice," Charlotte muttered, clambering off of the bed.

"You and I need to have a little talk," Gabe said, his eyes glinting with dark promise.

She grinned. "We can discuss it when you do my laundry for two months, O unlucky one."

"Gabe, you're not helping," Dana complained, glaring at him. "We were discussing important things before you breezed in and brought your…your Hoodlum, 'just one of the guys' vibes with you."

"What are you talking about?" he asked.

"I was talking to Charlotte about her future," Dana said, offhandedly gesturing toward the book on the bed. "You're distracting her. Can't you just wait in the hall?"

"Distracting her from what?" Gabe asked, then stopped as he glanced to where she'd gestured. "Oh, no. Not that."

"Not what?" Charlotte said, frowning.

"Tell me you're not going to read that!"

Charlotte saw where he was pointing and quickly

made a dash for it. Gabe dove onto the bed, grabbing the book at the exact moment she did.

"Let...me...see...this," he said, tugging stubbornly.

"Like hell I will!"

"I'm ready," Bella sang, opening the bathroom door, only to gasp in horror as she caught sight of her brother and her bridesmaid tussling. Dana simply shook her head. "What is going on here?"

Taking advantage of Gabe's momentary distraction, Charlotte made one last yank at the book. She managed to tug it away from him, but overbalanced. In a cloud of watered silk, she went flying over the edge of the bed, landing with a heavy thud.

"Got it," she crowed triumphantly, then rubbed her head. "Ouch."

Bella sighed. "When are you two going to grow up?"

"Never," Gabe replied. "We're going to be chasing each other with squirt guns when we're in a rest home together. Come on, angel, I'll give you a hand up."

With muscular grace, he helped her off of the floor. Then he promptly snatched the book out of her hand.

"You dirty..."

"*The Guide.* Oh, good grief," he snickered, thumbing through pages and reading passages aloud. "Be dramatic, but be demure. You're a woman. *Be* a woman." He guffawed, ignoring the trio of women glaring at him venomously. "What else would you be? A hamster?"

"Oh, give me that," Charlotte snapped, yanking it back out of his hands.

"You don't want to be Mrs. Right in one year, anyway," Gabe said with certainty, then narrowed his eyes. "Do you?"

"Of course not," Charlotte replied by instinct, then stopped. Well, it wasn't really a matter of wanting to be. It was a matter of knowing she *couldn't* be. Still, did she want to be?

Yes, a tiny voice inside her whispered, surprising her. In one year or one decade, she wanted to be right for someone. She wanted to find someone right for her.

"Charlotte might not think it's what she wants, but she hasn't had enough experience to say definitively," Dana said firmly. "She's got a lot going for her when she tries. If she'd just put her mind to it, she'd be a knockout. A real head-turner."

"Given a little time and a little effort," Bella added, crossing her arms, "I doubt it would take a whole year to find some guy who would fall all over himself to marry her!"

Charlotte felt a sudden burst of panic.

"And a gorgeous one, at that," Dana added enthusiastically, building momentum.

"She'd have him at her feet in a month," Bella said.

"Now, let's not get crazy here," Charlotte interjected, not liking the direction this was going at all.

"And she'd get a proposal in a matter of months, if she really went all out," Dana said, nodding. "Three months, easy!"

Gabe shook his head, throwing a casual arm around Charlotte's shoulders. "Why push her? Charlotte's my best friend, and I know her better than anyone. You can't tell me that she's going to read one stupid paperback, get a new hairdo or something, and suddenly turn into a *wife*. That's ludicrous."

Charlotte had been about to protest, also, but not in those words. "Not that I have any interest—"

"She's not even from the same planet as those

women that do *The Guide* thing," he continued. "I mean, the women who use that as a game plan go at it like pros. They've got the looks, the moves, the whole nine yards. They turn men into putty." He grinned at her. "We both know you're not like them, Charlie."

The three women stared at him in silence for a long moment. Charlotte was the first to recover.

"Thank you," Charlotte said, her voice frosty. She pushed his arm off of her. "Would you like me to turn the other cheek, so you can hit me with another backhanded compliment?"

"What? Oh, come on, angel," he said, tugging at one of her cockeyed curls with a look of amusement. "We're talking about a marriage proposal in three months. Let's get back to the same zip code as reality."

"I'm not saying it's what I *want*," she said, trying to maintain as much dignity as she could. "But if I really wanted Mr. Right, I could get him. I'm just happy with my life the way it is now, that's all."

"Really?" Gabe's eyes lit up, and Charlotte immediately mistrusted them. "And you actually believe that?"

Charlotte's temper flared, hot and dangerous. "Try me."

"No, thanks," he said, chuckling. "If we're going to bet, I'd like at least a minor challenge."

Charlotte's blood began to boil. She privately didn't think she was some skilled seductress, granted. Hearing him announce so easily that he *knew* she wasn't was something else entirely.

"You're on. I'll bet you ten bucks I could." It was stupid, but her pride pushed her to it. She was *single by choice,* and that was the lie she was swearing to. How dare he turn on her like this!

"Ten bucks? Seriously?" Gabe's eyes widened, then that damned amusement grew more pronounced. "Come on. It's not like we're betting on football here. Or who can hold their liquor better, for that matter."

Now her head was pounding. She wanted to smack that smug grin off his face. The words tumbled out before she could think about them. "One hundred dollars, Casanova. And I'll be wearing things that would make even you blush."

"That in itself would be worth betting on. Sometimes I think you were born in a sweatshirt," he said, his grin growing. "One hundred dollars is still child's play, angel. Maybe make it two months, and we'll talk."

"Two months," she agreed, her voice low. "And two hundred dollars."

Finally, some of his amusement slipped. "Charlie, come on now. You're getting in way over your head."

His patronizing tone threw gasoline on the fire. "Five hundred."

He was no longer smiling. In fact, his face looked grim. "This is ridiculous. I'm not going to listen to one more—"

"One thousand dollars."

Dana was staring at her, speechless. Bella's mouth had fallen open.

"One thousand dollars says I get a marriage proposal in two months," she repeated, staring at Gabe's face as if there was no one else in the room. Her hands bunched in fists at her sides. "One thousand dollars says you don't think I can do it. That no man would have me."

He paused, then looked at her shrewdly. "Only if you make it one month."

He waited for her to back down.

She didn't waver. "Deal."

"You don't want to do this, Charlie," he said, giving her a little shake. "You're losing your mind!"

"And you're losing your nerve," she said, smiling coldly. "Put up or shut up, Gabe."

They stood toe to toe for a long, maddening minute. Gabe studied her, not blinking. Then he smiled, a megawatt-bright smile.

"You're bluffing…and I'm calling you." Battle lit his eyes, and he held out a hand. "You're on."

With a swift motion, Charlotte grabbed his hand in a hard shake.

He stared down at her for a moment longer, then shook his head. "Fine. I'm going to go downstairs and tell the men you're taking your time," he said to Bella. "I'm sure you're going to want to stay a few more minutes to work on a game plan. That is, before Charlotte drops a grand in a month."

Giving Charlotte one last smug wink, he strode out the door.

"Oh, my God," Bella breathed. "I can't believe you did that!"

"What's done is done," Dana said, nodding with approval. "We've only got one month. A shopping trip, first thing. No, wait. My hairdresser! And maybe a facial…"

"Facial, nothing. Full day of spa treatment," Bella said, diving for her purse and producing a business card. "I'll be back from Hawaii in exactly two weeks. You guys take care of clothes and makeup. I'll work out a strategy."

"One thousand dollars," Dana said, glancing at Charlotte with a curious gleam of pride. "Unbelievable."

2

EIGHT O'CLOCK the next morning, the persistent sound of her doorbell jarred Charlotte from a restless sleep. She stumbled out of bed, muttering and rubbing at her sleep-sandy eyes. "If it's Gabe, you might as well know I decided to forfeit," she called. "I must have been insane. Would you just leave me to wallow in my singleness in peace?"

"Not a chance," a muffled female voice countered. "It's Dana. Open up."

Charlotte groaned. Dana. Even worse. She unlatched the chain and cautiously pulled the door open.

"Well?" Dana looked far too enthusiastic about being up this early on a Sunday morning. "Today is the first day of the new you, Charlotte Taylor. Are you ready?"

"What are you? Captain of the matrimonial cheerleading squad?" Charlotte shuffled over to the kitchen and turned on her coffeemaker. No way was she facing one of Dana's makeover speeches without caffeine. "Besides, I'm not going through with this. I did a lot of thinking, and I'm going to get Gabe to just drop the whole thing. I don't really need to prove anything...."

"Oh no you don't," Dana countered, frowning at Charlotte as she unslung a fair-size bag from her shoulder. She started piling small jars, bottles and tubes on the kitchen table. "On any other bet, I'd

Charlotte gritted her teeth. "I've never lost a bet with Gabe without a fight. Now, pipe down," she ordered, a viselike grip on the paperback. "I'm trying to read here!"

probably be trying to stop you myself—you two manage to come up with some fairly idiotic ones—but this time, I'm all for it. I've waited ten years for you to do something with those buried gorgeous looks of yours. There is no chance in heck I'm letting you off that easily.''

Charlotte eyed the supplies warily. ''What's all this for?''

Dana smiled. ''This is step one.''

''Step one?'' Charlotte picked up one of the bottles. The label was in Norwegian and most of the ingredients had eighteen syllables. ''How many steps are there?''

''That depends on how cooperative you are.''

Dana proceeded to get a box of oatmeal out of the pantry, then mixed some with water in a bowl.

''I wasn't planning on eating breakfast,'' Charlotte groused, pouring herself a mugful of coffee, ''so I hope that's not for me.''

''This isn't for your insides. This is for your outsides.'' Dana grabbed one of the bottles, added some of its green liquid to the bowl, then studied the resultant mixture. ''It's also going to get a little messy. Here, stir this.''

Charlotte stirred, then gaped as Dana produced a clear plastic tarp from her bag and laid it out on the living room floor. ''What is *that* for?''

Dana didn't answer. Opening the front door and walking to the deck, she grabbed one of the forest-green plastic chairs and dragged it inside. ''Here you go. Sit down.''

Charlotte took a quick chug out of her coffee mug before Dana plunked her down in the chair, ignoring Charlotte's startled yelp. Charlotte tried to frown at her friend, but wasn't able to turn far enough in the chair to see her. "Okay, this has gone from annoying to painful, Dana."

Dana took a breath, and Charlotte could feel that intent, "helping friend" stare of hers. "Listen to me. I don't mean to be pushy, or rude, but I'm going to flat-out say it. Honey, you need help…and for the first time since high school, we're going to make sure you get it."

Charlotte gritted her teeth. Apparently, the time for wheedling and not-so-subtle nudges from her friends had passed. Dana and Bella had gone to war. "I know I haven't seemed—"

"Hush. Let me finish." Dana's voice was firm. "I don't mean to play amateur psychologist here, but being raised by your dad alone all those years couldn't have made it easy for you. Bella and I did everything we could, but even I know two girls aren't going to replace a mother."

"You both loved me and did what you thought was best at the time." Which Charlotte had really appreciated, even if she often chafed under their efforts. "It wasn't easy, but see? I managed just fine."

"But you're *not* managing. That's my whole point." Dana sighed with obvious frustration. "You've tolerated us, you've humored us, but you're stubbornly convinced that you're not pretty and that you're not going to find a man who will fall in love with you. You're just hiding behind that 'just one of the guys' facade. Well, your days of hiding are over." Dana craned her head to stare directly into Charlotte's face. "And don't do that chin thing at me, either."

Charlotte blinked. "What chin thing?"

"The 'I'll tune back in when she says something I want to hear' chin thing."

Charlotte sighed. "Okay. I'm listening. What exactly is it you want me to do?"

"Really try at this. Give it your best shot."

"I'm not hiding, Dana. I...okay, *maybe* I could be a little braver in the social arena. But frankly, I'm happy with my life as it is. I don't *need* to date. I don't *need* to change my appearance. Why can't people be happy with me the way I am?"

Dana sighed. "Someday, a man is going to love you for just who you are, honey. I promise that. But if you're so happy with your life, why were you so sad at Bella's wedding?" Her eyes bore into Charlotte like lasers. "And don't tell me it was your hangover. We've known each other much too long."

That was the problem with having childhood friends. They read you like a book, Charlote thought, resigned.

"We'd leave you alone if we knew you were really happy," Dana said, giving her a quick, hard hug. "But we're not letting you just settle for a life of mediocrity without a fight. If you'd let that outer beauty catch up with your inner beauty, I know you'd find the right person for you. I just know it."

"Beauty? Me?" Charlotte's voice cracked. "What have you been smoking?"

Dana huffed impatiently. "One step at a time. Right now, the body comes first. We'll work on attitude soon, though."

She lifted the bowl in front of Charlotte, then grabbed a handful of the oatmeal mixture.

"Dana," Charlotte warned, "no way am I letting you turn my face into cooked cereal...arrrgh." She was silenced as Dana mercilessly glopped the thick, pasty stuff on her face. She shut her eyes and faced the inevitable.

"Sit still. This is just the beginning. I've got a hair appointment for you at twelve, and get ready for a full afternoon of shopping...."

Dana continued to burble on happily as she out-lined her grand scheme for Charlotte's transformation. Charlotte fought tears as the list grew longer.

There was no way she could turn down their help. If it had been anyone else, she would say exactly where they could stow their bright ideas and make-over agendas. But it was her two oldest friends... friends who had made room for her at holidays, friends who had clapped and cheered at the college graduation her father had missed, dying two years ear-lier of cancer. She loved them enough to put up with their pushing, prodding and relentless mothering. She'd die for them if they asked.

But dying was one thing, her mind countered stub-bornly. Making a complete fool out of herself for the second time in her life was something else!

"Charlotte, have you heard a word I've said?"

Charlotte was jolted out of her thoughts. "What?"

Dana chuckled, then walked to the kitchen to put the bowl down in the sink. "I've been outlining your beauty agenda. I'm sure this is overwhelming to you right now, but I know you. You're going to work harder at this than at anything in your life."

Charlotte turned, only to have her head spun as Dana grabbed her hair and made thoughtful noises. "What in the world gives you that impression?" Charlotte asked, puzzled.

"That bet," Dana said, reaching for another jar. "You've never done less than two hundred percent to win a bet with Gabe. When you two shook hands, I could have kissed him!"

The temper that had gotten Charlotte into this mess sprung to life. "Oh, me too," Charlotte said acidly. "My best friend tells me in no uncertain terms that I not only lack the looks but the outright talent to get a man. Yeah. What a pal."

Dana laughed, then smoothed a fistful of clay onto Charlotte's head. It felt cold and squishy, and dribbles of it crawled down her neck. She squirmed uncomfortably in her seat.

"Well, now's your chance to prove him wrong. Really go all out. Honestly," Dana said, massaging the clay into Charlotte's scalp, "forget the bet. If you don't get a guy in one month, I will not only be shocked, I will throw in the towel for good. I'll give up my title as both matchmaker and makeover-er."

The sharp retort that Charlotte had been about to make died on her lips. "Really? You'd give it up?"

"Full money-back guarantee, and I'll never bug you on the subject again," Dana said, popping a clear plastic shower cap over Charlotte's mud-laden head. "I'll make sure Bella doesn't, either. I have that much confidence in you."

Charlotte didn't say anything. A diplomatic way to get her friends to leave her alone? After only one month?

Suddenly, the bet with Gabe didn't seem like such a horrible thing after all. Sure, she'd have to figure out a way around the thousand dollar part, but otherwise the rest of it was a piece of cake. She'd let the girls curl, crimp, color and coordinate to their hearts' contents. Then she'd lose, they'd concede, and she could finally get on with her life with some modicum of peace. It was perfect!

Suddenly, *she* felt like kissing Gabe. This backhanded bet was just what she was looking for!

"Well, then," Charlotte said, beaming her first real smile of the morning. "Let the transformation begin!"

"What transformation?" Gabe's voice called from the front door.

Dana let out a startled little yip. Charlotte, on the

other hand, made a break for the bathroom as soon as she heard him. Unfortunately, her foot slipped on the slick plastic tarp. She sprawled out on the floor, facedown and bottom up.

"Well, well," Gabe drawled, grating on every single one of Charlotte's nerves. "There's a sight you don't see every day."

"And thank God for that," Charlotte muttered, getting up slowly. "Don't you knock? And what are you doing here this early in the morning, anyway?"

"In all the years I've known you, I've never knocked if your door is open," he said, shrugging. "As far as why I'm here, there's a football game on in half an hour. I haven't gone food shopping yet, and I thought, my good buddy Charlotte always has something..."

"Please. Just help yourself," Charlotte said sarcastically, rolling her eyes.

"Don't mind if I do," Gabe agreed, helping himself to a mug of coffee and rooting through her refrigerator for a bagel. "You seem particularly grumpy this morning. Could it be because our good friend Dana here got you up early, or because she spackled your face?"

Dana and Charlotte both glared at him, and he laughed. "Sorry. I guess it's a girl thing."

"It's more like a bet thing," Dana snapped, gathering her makeover supplies and piling them back into her bag.

"Bet?" Gabe pretended to mull it over. "I seem to remember something about that. One grand, one month, and from the looks of it, a whole lot of oatmeal." Gabe winked at Charlotte. "Think you'll be able to wash all that off by Thursday? We've got one serious poker night going on at my house, and I don't want you covering your famous poker face with that goop. You'll scare the guys.''

''The only thing they'll be scared of is making their rent after I've cleaned them out,'' Charlotte boasted.

''Oh no you don't,'' Dana cut in, frowning at Gabe before turning back to Charlotte. ''From here on out, Thursdays through Sundays are designated date nights. You're booked.''

Charlotte took a deep breath. Just one tiny, minuscule month, she reminded herself. ''Okay, coach.''

The teasing look washed off Gabe's face. ''Okay?'' His gray eyes widened. ''Just like that? You'd ditch poker night to wait for…for some *guy?*''

''No,'' Charlotte corrected him sweetly, ''I'm ditching poker night to *go out with* some guy.''

Gabe scowled at her, but Dana laughed. ''That's my girl! Now, I've got to confirm that massage and full body wrap I've got scheduled for you tonight at the spa. Where did you leave your phone?''

''It's in the bedroom,'' Charlotte said absently. Dana made a beeline for it, reciting her makeover to-do list as she went.

Now was the perfect time to maybe negotiate the bet from a thousand down to something more reasonable. She might have to swallow a little pride, but it would be worth it. With Gabe's help, the four weeks could fly by. Without it…

''You can't be serious about this,'' Gabe muttered before she could say anything.

It wasn't so much what he said. It was the *tone* that immediately put her back up. ''Why not?''

''Because it's insane!'' Gabe said, running his hand through his hair in a trademark gesture of frustration. ''I was just kidding, for pity's sake. I figured even if you did agree, one week with the makeover fascists would have you crying uncle.''

Charlotte almost smiled at that one, until she heard his next sentence.

"Besides, you don't really want to find Mr. Right. You wouldn't know what do with him if you found him. You're not like those *Guide* women at all." His voice rang with certainty. "Think about it. You, trying to snare some unsuspecting man and drag him home by the hair?"

"Actually, I was planning on just wearing something see-through at my front door and luring them in," Charlotte snapped back, irritated by his amusement. "The kind of men I'm after would probably be too heavy for me to drag."

Gabe growled, then took a deep breath, apparently deciding to try a different approach. "There's nothing wrong with the way you are, and you shouldn't let them try to change you," he said, his voice more serious. "I thought you liked your life the way it was. What's so wrong about hanging out with us guys, anyway? We never hassle you about changing. We don't care *what* you look like!"

Translation: she could be the ugliest mud-beast to walk the face of the earth, but she'd always be "their Charlie."

"So you dress grubby..." he continued.

"Okay, stop right there." Swallowing her pride was one thing. Choking to death on it was another! "Before that foot becomes permanently lodged in your throat, stop trying to convince me. My mind's made up. *I'm going through with this bet.*"

This was not the way to convince him to help her, she realized. But the way he was acting, she didn't *want* his help. He wasn't pitying her, exactly, but he was...excusing her, somehow. It was worse than being pitied by the girls. He deserved a little payback, even if she knew she couldn't win. She might not ever look "beautiful," but he'd definitely think twice before he used the term *grubby* again!

"I may not look like much now, Gabe," she said, with anger-induced bravado, "but I swear, I'm going to look like the goddess of love when you're signing that check."

"Better watch that mud pack, Venus," he countered, leaning closer to her, a wicked grin on his face. "I hate to tell you, but you've got terra-cotta coating your neck. And there's a cozy scoop of oatmeal between your..."

He started laughing too hard to speak, cutting off his sentence, and he raised a finger to point.

Charlotte saw red. Snatching up one of the pillows from her overstuffed couch, she side-armed it at him, catching him straight in his chuckling mouth. He grabbed the little plastic chair as a shield as she pelted him with the rest of her ammunition.

Still steaming, she glanced around for something else to throw. Then she noticed the unholy gleam in Gabe's eyes as he put the chair down.

She felt a brief pang of panic as she realized his intentions. "Gabe," she protested, holding a hand up. "Now, let's not be hasty here. I'm your best friend...."

He picked up an armful of pillows and grinned.

"Ga-a-a-abe!" She gave one last, desperate cry as he began to bombard her. He was blocking off the entrance to both her room and the bathroom, and his aim was wickedly on target. With a scream, she bolted toward her front hallway, with Gabe in full pursuit.

"Dammit, Gabe!" Trapped, she threw open her front door and ran out, his deep, rolling laughter dogging her every step. She made a dash for the side of the house. She hoped the garden hose was out so she

could give him a nice cold blast, when instead she
ran smack into a broad, muscular chest.

"Oof," she uttered, landing on the soft grass of the
side yard with a thump.

"Oops! Sorry," a deep male voice intoned, with
an undercurrent of amusement. "Are you all right?"

She looked up. A golden, gorgeous Adonis was
staring down at her. His bare, golden tanned chest
emerged from what looked like a low-slung pair of
Dockers. She gaped, horrified.

"Are you all right, miss?" Adonis repeated, looking less amused now and more worried. He also
looked vaguely familiar. She shook off the thought.
If she knew somebody this good-looking, she'd remember it! "I didn't mean to knock you over," he
apologized. He offered her a hand to tug her up.

She stared at it. Of all the days for this sort of thing
to happen to her, why *today,* when she looked like
this?

Gabe suddenly emerged, pillows in each hand, yell-
ing like a Comanche. He stopped, mid war cry, as he
noticed the new participant and saw Charlotte on the
ground.

"What happened?" Gabe asked, quickly dropping
the pillows and falling to his knees by Charlotte's
side. "Angel, are you all right?"

She grimaced at him. Did she *look* all right?

Adonis cleared his throat. "I'm sorry. I...she was
running around the house, and I didn't know she was
coming, and we bumped into each other. I think
maybe she got the wind knocked out of her."

Charlotte groaned and pushed herself up to her feet,
glad that at least the oatmeal covered her blush. "No,
I'm fine," she muttered. *Of course I'm fine. Adonis
moves in next door to me, and I run at him like a
stampeding wildebeest.* "I guess I should have been

more careful of where I was going, but I didn't know anyone lived here."

Adonis smiled, dimples pitting his cheeks. "No problem. I just moved in. A friend of mine owns this place, but he's subletting it to me for a while. I've always liked Manhattan Beach. It's fun." He winked at her, a gesture that reminded her of Gabe. "Always something crazy going on."

"This isn't what you think," she protested weakly.

Gabe was obviously enjoying the predicament she'd landed in. "What, exactly, do you think he thought this was?"

"You…" she began, only to be stopped by Adonis's laugh.

"Do you two live next door, then?" Adonis glanced curiously at her house.

"I live there," Charlotte answered, giving Gabe a quick glare. "The comedian over here doesn't. He just stopped by to make my life miserable."

"Oh," Adonis said slowly, looking back at her. "I thought you two were married."

"Us?" Charlotte's eyebrows jumped up, causing crackling oatmeal to sprinkle into her eyes. She blinked hard.

"Not just no, but *hell* no," Gabe said. "Marriage is miserable enough by itself. Why would I compound it by marrying her?"

This time, she aimed a kick at him. He dodged it, still grinning.

"Oh," Adonis said, smiling broadly. He offered his hand to her. "Then let's get introduced. I'm Jack Landor."

"Jack Landor? *Society* magazine's Most Eligible Bachelor in America?" She laughed. "Sure you are. And I'm Glinda, the Good Witch of the North."

He laughed, a deep, rough laugh that appealed.

When he smiled, he *did* sort of resemble Jack Landor, she noted.

"Well, Glinda, you can just call me Jack."

"Hi, Jack," Gabe said, stepping slightly in front of Charlotte and putting his hand out. Jack had to release Charlotte's hand to shake Gabe's. "I'm Gabe Dono-frio."

"I'm Charlotte Taylor," Charlotte added, nudging Gabe a little. He didn't budge.

"Hi, Charlotte," Jack said, smiling. He added a nod to Gabe. Charlotte smirked when Gabe finally moved aside a little.

Gabe smiled back at her, too smugly for her peace of mind. His gaze shifted downward a little, and his smile widened, amusement dancing in his eyes. She tried to track his line of vision. What was so funny?

Abruptly, she remembered the comment that had started all of this. She had oatmeal between her *what?*

"Well, welcome to the neighborhood, Jack," she said quickly. Hoping that she wasn't nestling cereal between her breasts, she smiled sheepishly and added, "I've got to go slip into something less, er, edible."

Jack smiled back, this time with a hint of heat. "Oh, don't bother on my account."

She paused for a moment.

That sounded like a come-on.

Shaking her head, Charlotte laughed, waved and walked back up toward her house. Of course it wasn't a come-on. Adonis, hitting on the oatmeal mud girl? She'd been out of the dating scene way too long if she could entertain a crazy idea like that!

Gabe trailed behind her, pillows in hand, but with no obvious intention of throwing them, thankfully. They walked into the house together. Dana waited for them in the living room, a horrified expression on her face.

"I can't believe you just did that," Dana said, her fingers tugging at her short red hair. She'd obviously been spying from the bedroom window. "Did you see that guy?"

"Couldn't miss him," Gabe said sourly, before Charlotte could answer. "He's Jack Landor."

Dana's eyes bugged. "No way."

"Way." Gabe plunked down on the couch. "And he was hitting on Charlotte."

"No *way!*" Dana threw a quick hug around Charlotte's shoulders, then just as quickly pulled back, rubbing at some clay that had gotten on her sleeve. "He hit on you? Looking like, um, that?"

"Coated in oatmeal and mud, you mean?" Charlotte gave an exasperated sigh. "He couldn't take his eyes off of me. I'm literally like no other woman he's ever seen before…or ever hopes to see again, I'm sure." She frowned at Gabe, kicking at the feet that he'd propped up on her coffee table. "Gabe's just pulling your leg, Dana. Jack Landor wouldn't be interested in me in a million years, and besides, I'm not even convinced that Adonis really *was* Jack Landor. Either way, that guy was not coming on to me!"

"Adonis?" Gabe repeated, frowning.

"What do you mean, he wasn't Jack Landor?" Dana persisted.

"He wasn't that good-looking," Gabe interrupted, standing up. "Are you interested in him or something? Because I think he's a little out of your league, Charlotte. I mean, I know you're taking this bet seriously and all, but you don't want to rush into anything."

"Right. That does it." Charlotte tugged the plastic cap off of her head. "Dana, I'll see you at the hairdresser's. Gabe, go to the supermarket, then go home. I'm going to take a shower. And we are not going to talk about oatmeal, mud packs or Jack Landor ever again, are we clear?''

Dana smiled. "See you at twelve."

Gabe got up, following Charlotte to the bathroom door. "Need help scrubbing off your back? I'm sure I could dig up a volunteer next door."

She slammed the bathroom door in his face and turned the shower on, full blast. Feeling the oatmeal run off her face under the pounding spray, she had one thought...

She might not win *this* bet, but the next time Gabe saw her, he wouldn't know what hit him. She'd stake her life savings on it.

3

BY THURSDAY, GABE was sick of being put off for Charlotte's "makeover agenda." She wouldn't see him, barely even had time to talk to him. Now he had only one goal: getting her to give up this stupid bet, for her own good.

He pulled his sleek black Mustang convertible into the parking lot of Howes Design, jetting into the nearest parking space. Getting Charlotte to do anything was difficult. Getting her to do something for her own good was damn near impossible.

"I am such an idiot," he muttered under his breath, retrieving the bouquet of white roses he'd gotten for her. Charlotte was a sucker for flowers. Two dozen red roses had saved his butt when he'd accidentally cracked her car's back window last year with a practical joke, he remembered with a smile.

Somehow, he doubted he'd get off the hook that easily this time. Once he and Charlotte shook hands on a bet, she was like a ton of cement: hard, completely set and impossible to budge.

He had handled Saturday badly, he realized. Even if she wouldn't believe it, he had been trying to help her. He knew how pushy his sister could get, and she had been after Charlotte for years, trying to "girl-ify" her. He was just trying to help Charlotte stop them, he thought logically. Then she'd gotten that fire in her eyes, and he'd indulged in pricking her temper. He knew he shouldn't get as much of a kick out of it as he did, but when Charlotte sparked, he couldn't help but react. He loved watching her go to any lengths to beat him at whatever it was they were shaking on. Besides, he'd thought she was bluffing, and he wasn't about to knuckle under if she was. It wasn't until he'd seen her the next morning that he realized everything the bet entailed.

What if she did meet some guy, like that jerk she'd dated in design school? The guy had turned into a psychotic Pygmalion, trying to turn Charlotte in as his final project. Gabe had just graduated himself and was looking forward to spending more time with Charlotte…they hadn't been close when he was in high school, but when he'd moved away to college on the East Coast, he realized he missed the tomboy brat who lived around the corner. But instead, she'd spent all of her time with her boyfriend until the jerk dumped her, and she'd wept on Gabe's shoulder and told him the story she couldn't tell the girls: how the guy had been trying to change her, how he'd said he'd given up because "the project was only as good as the materials…and you're not good enough."

She'd then made Gabe promise not to kill the guy, a promise Gabe still regretted.

If Charlotte went all out on this crazy bet, who knew what sort of lunatic she'd hook up with, just to show him she could.

And if she got married, where would that put me in her life?

He ignored the tiny voice that had been poking at him since Sunday morning. He'd make her see reason, no problem. From what he'd seen, she wasn't unhappy with her life. She always seemed happy when she was with him, anyway…except for the wedding. But that was probably just a fluke, a mood thing. As he'd said to Brad, weddings did weird things to women. And if he knew Charlotte, he knew she didn't want to be anybody's Mrs. Right.

He'd make sure she remembered that.

"Say" came a woman's voice from the front door. "Are you going to come in, or are you just going to loiter for the rest of the afternoon by our front door?"

"Huh?" He was startled out of his thoughts. "What?"

Wanda, the receptionist at Howes Design, smiled at him as she held open the door. "Those flowers for me, handsome?"

He smiled back. "No, they're a peace offering for Charlotte. Is she in?"

A strange look crossed Wanda's face. "She sure is." Gabe followed Wanda through the door into the air-conditioned lobby. "So. Are you what happened to her?"

"What happened to her?" he echoed. "What do you mean?"

"She looks strange, Gabe," Wanda said conspiratorially, leaning a little too close to him. "I mean, I've never seen her look like this before. It's weird."

He groaned. "Oh, no."

Wanda shifted gears, her smile turning seductive. She was close enough that her red curls brushed against his shoulder. "So what are you doing this weekend, handsome?"

"Penance," he muttered. Then he added more clearly, "Thanks, Wanda."

He hurried down the hallway. What could Charlotte have done now? God, he hoped she hadn't unearthed those bizarre designs that jerk had concocted...pastel granny dresses with combat boots. Or was it worse? Pinstriped straightjackets with sensible shoes? Leopard prints? Lederhosen? Or had she just given up completely and shaved her head?

Taking a deep breath, he courageously slapped on a big smile before throwing the door open and entering, flowers first.

He froze.

Charlotte barely glanced up, smiling tiredly. "Hey there. Come on in. I just need to finish up this sketch...this client is a nightmare. I've been working like a demon all morning."

He felt like somebody had punched him in the stomach. "Um, sure," he said slowly, wishing he could stop staring. "You look...good."

She looked up at him for a second, with a little smirk. "Damn me with faint praise."

Whatever he had been expecting, it wasn't this. She looked strange, all right. Strangely alluring, strangely striking. Strangely beautiful.

Her straggly long hair had been cut to her shoulders, falling in graceful waves. Something else was different about it, he noted. It was darker, more chestnut, maybe. She wore it pushed back a little, showing off that swan's neck of hers. It suited those high cheekbones nicely.

He blinked. When the hell had he noticed she had high cheekbones?

Her hazel eyes were huge, glowing with life. "Gabe? Hello-o-o, Gabe." Her smile was shy and self-conscious. "That bad, huh?"

It was the smile that snapped him out of it. No matter what she looked like, that smile was pure Charlotte...that little softness that took the sting out of her sharpest, hippest remarks. "Nah," he said, regaining his equilibrium. "I was just mentally balancing my checkbook to see if I could clear a grand, or if I'd have to raid my savings."

She laughed, showing off a rosy little blush that added life to her clear porcelain complexion. If this kept up, he thought desperately, he'd start writing a sonnet about her. He thrust out the flowers almost aggressively. "For you," he muttered.

The blush deepened a little. She was wearing some kind of dusty rose lipstick, and her lips looked full and generous as they curved into a delighted smile. "I didn't get anything for you," she joked, her voice low and husky.

Her voice had always been like that, hadn't it? So why did his pulse suddenly rev up like an engine at the Indy 500?

Then she got up and took a vase off of the tall bookcase behind her worktable.

He thought he'd been shocked. Now he was beyond shocked. He felt like someone had taken a sledgehammer to his chest as he tried without success to take a breath.

She wasn't wearing her usual baggy jeans. Instead, she wore a short, flirty sundress in a fragile pastel pink that floated like a cloud around her body. The neck scooped to reveal the gentle swell of her breasts. And she was wearing strappy white sandals. With *heels.* He wasn't sure what weird equation of physics made heels do what they did to women's legs, but they were acting in overdrive on Charlotte's. Her legs were long and luscious, just the way he liked…

This is Charlotte you're ogling.

The thought brought him up short.

She paused in her impromptu flower arranging, pulling out the little white flag he'd tucked into them. She turned, tapping one foot as she smirked at him. "So what's this for?"

"Unconditional surrender," he murmured, wrenching his gaze up from her legs and wondering just when the hell he had lost control of the situation. "On both our parts. Let's just call this stupid bet off, Charlie."

He watched as her face turned hard, and sighed. It just wasn't going to be that easy.

"So what brought this on, Gabe?" She walked over to the drawing table, her heels clicking viciously against the hardwood floor.

"What do you think?"

One of her finely arched eyebrows quirked up. "Let's see. Because you don't think I have a prayer of doing anything but making a fool of myself with this bet?"

"I never said that," he interrupted. "I just don't want you to get hurt."

"Translation—you think I'm going to get hurt because I'm not the sort of woman that men go bonkers over."

Until today, he thought. He couldn't remember exactly what he'd thought before today. "I never thought you were ugly," he said instead, more sharply than he'd intended.

"Oh, really? Then what did you think?"

He opened his mouth, then shut it, reconsidering. "You're sweet, and nice, and funny. You're a mean poker player and a great quarterback. You're brilliant at your job...."

"Oh, and all that keeps my organizer filled with dates," she said, breaking in sarcastically. "My looks, Gabe. How did you think I *looked?*"

He sighed. "You're my best friend. How am I supposed to know? I don't think of my friends that way!"

"That is the biggest cop-out I've ever heard."

"I knew it. You've only been doing this for a few days, and already you're turning all girly on me," he

said with asperity. "Looking at you, hearing you talk,
I know this is a bad idea. Besides, do you know the
kind of men that are prowling around these days? You
don't know what you're getting into!"

Her eyes blazed. "I can take care of myself, thanks
very much. I have for years. You don't need to worry
about me!"

"I've been worrying about you for years," Gabe
raged back at her. "And that was when you were still
in your right mind!"

They stood there for a long moment, their words
like fallen swords between them. Before either could
break the silence, the phone rang. They both jumped,
startled.

Charlotte snatched up the receiver. "Yes?"

Gabe took a deep breath. Okay, he'd botched that
one thoroughly. He'd meant to be convincing, suavely
persuasive. Then he'd taken one look at her and his
well-laid plans went straight out the window. Hopefully, he could still salvage the situation. Once she
got off of the phone, he'd try to be a little more
smooth.

"Glinda, Good Witch of the North?" Her eyes
widened, bewildered, then closed. "Oh, my God. Hi,
yes, I'm sorry. This is Charlotte Taylor. I didn't mean
to snap like that, I'm just in the middle of something.
Is this Jack?"

Any thoughts Gabe had of peacemaking disappeared. Jack Landor? What was he doing, calling
Charlotte here? And what did he want?

Gabe stopped himself, midthought. Oh, he could
guess what good old Jack wanted, all right.

"Hi, Jack. Yes, I've recovered fully from this
weekend. You're a brave man, not to run off screaming at the sight of me. I'm sure I was something to
see." She chuckled, halfheartedly. "What? Oh, that."

She laughed again, and Gabe saw a deep red blush creep across her face. "You weren't supposed to notice that blop of oatmeal there."

Gabe saw purple. Suddenly, he felt the overwhelming urge to hit something, preferably Jack. That lech!

"Hmm… So, you want a local person's advice on what the hot spots are in Manhattan Beach, huh? Well, I guess I could help you a little. I know several excellent restaurants, a ton of sports bars and a few dance clubs…what?" Gabe suppressed the urge to hit the speaker button and hear what was causing the shocked look on her face. "Um, I'm, uh, not sure. Today's Thursday, right? No, I don't have any other plans tonight.…"

Gabe clenched his fist. The man was railroading Charlotte into a date. The nerve of the guy!

"What? Your other line? Sure, I can hold," Charlotte said. She looked over at Gabe, covering the mouthpiece. "It's Jack Landor. I'm holding."

"Breathlessly," Gabe growled. "You're not thinking of going out with that character, are you?"

"Well, I hadn't…" she started, then stopped, her eyes flashing. "Why shouldn't I?"

"He could be an ax murderer for all you know!"

"He's Jack Landor!" Charlotte exclaimed. "At this point, he's getting so famous he's lucky to go to the bathroom with privacy, much less kill anyone!"

"My point exactly!" Gabe yelled back, then stopped. No, that wasn't his point at all. Normally, he had a lot more logic on his side, but his anger had seriously shorted out the better part of his brain. "All I'm saying is, you're not thinking this through. He's big-league, he's famous…and you've got that damned bet on your brain. Why would you want to go out with some celebrity freak show otherwise? Think about it!"

Her eyes narrowed, like shards of hazel ice. ''Or, more to the point, why would he want to go out with me?''

Gabe grimaced. ''Don't go there, Charlotte. I swear.''

''Jack? Hi.'' Her voice rang with an edge of steel. ''I'd love to go out to dinner with you tonight. I think we should try Blue Moon, over on Manhattan Beach Boulevard. It's sort of nouveau Italian, and the food is terrific. How does seven sound?'' She paused for a moment, listening. ''Perfect. Well, yes, you *do* know where I live. We can just walk there, it's very close. Sure. I'll see you then.'' She placed the phone gently in its cradle, then stared at it. ''I have a date with Jack Landor. Tonight.''

''How did he get your work number?'' Gabe asked pugnaciously. ''Answer me that, why don't you!''

''Gabe, I don't have to answer you one little thing.'' She pointed to the door. ''What's more, I think this conversation has gone about as far as it can go. Get out, Gabe.''

''We're not finished,'' he warned.

''We will be if you keep it up. Out!''

''Fine!'' He couldn't resist slamming the door, an action that caused several heads to pop up like gophers over the low cubicle walls in the main room. He scowled at them. They disappeared rapidly.

So she was going out with Jack Landor tonight, huh? Thought she could ''take care of herself.'' Well, he'd just see about that. In fact, if she was so hell-bent on proving what a *Guide* girl she was, he'd show her exactly how insane those women could be.

Tonight, he planned on showing her that nobody knew more about dating—or winning—than Gabe Donofrio.

HOURS LATER, CHARLOTTE was still raw from her exchange with Gabe. Imagine him stomping in here like a caveman and claiming that she couldn't take care of herself. And the ridiculous accusation that she wouldn't be safe with Jack. If that was the best he could do to win that stupid bet, she'd win by default!

She threw her design stuff in her catchall basket, too stressed to indulge in her usual calming ritual of organization. Now, thanks to his meddling, his pressuring and his big mouth, she was going on a date in two hours.

Suddenly, the thought hit home.

Date.

She was going on a date.

In two hours.

With the most eligible man in America.

Oh, no. What had she just agreed to?

She walked out, dazed, not surprised to see that most of the other designers had taken an early Thursday to enjoy the Indian summer weather. A lot of them had been working weekends to land the Kensington account and deserved a little break before the next big project. A project she'd still be working on if she hadn't agreed to this dinner date with Adonis, she thought, getting more anxious. Maybe she should cancel. He'd understand if it was for work, wouldn't he?

Or maybe she could call him and tell him she was sick. He'd have to understand that. In fact, she felt like throwing up right now.

Wanda was just shutting down the switchboard for the night when Charlotte walked through the lobby. Wanda surveyed Charlotte, her lips bowing into a tiny, pointed smile. "That friend of yours went tearing out of here this afternoon like he wanted to kill somebody. What happened?"

Charlotte sighed. Wanda was the biggest busybody in the building. She also went through men the way kids go through Pez candies. "He doesn't approve of my taste in dates," she muttered darkly.

"You've got a date?" Wanda's ultramarine eyes rounded. This was probably the juiciest gossip the woman would get all week. "Well, that explains it."

"Explains what?"

"The changes." Wanda's well-manicured ruby nails gestured to Charlotte's dress. "The get-up. You know."

"Maybe I just wanted a change," Charlotte protested.

Wanda gave her a pitying look. "Come on, now. It's just us girls here." The two walked out of the building, Wanda punching in the alarm code as they left. "Nobody goes through all that trouble unless there's a manhunt involved. It's not like you'd look like that normally."

"Is there something wrong with the way I look?" Charlotte said, half-defensive, half-worried. She gave herself a surreptitious glance in the reflection of the glass doors. Dana and the woman at the store had said that the dress was flattering, but she herself hadn't been that crazy about it. Pastels weren't her thing. Darn it, she just wasn't sure about this stuff!

"Oh, no, of course not. It's sort of…well, it's very different," Wanda said graciously. "And I've often said that you needed a change. I just wasn't expecting one quite so radical."

"Radical?" Charlotte didn't think it was that big a deal. Okay, maybe she did, but she wasn't expecting everyone she knew to think it was that big a deal.

"But maybe radical is just what you need," Wanda continued. Her skyscraper heels clacked on the asphalt as they walked to their respective cars.

If I walked that way, I'd dislocate one of my hips. Charlotte shook off the thought. "What do you mean?"

"From the extreme change, I'd say you must be on a husband-hunt. And that calls for the heavy artillery." Wanda smirked as she strutted over to her red convertible. "Desperate times call for desperate measures, right?"

Charlotte stopped by Jellybean, the nickname she'd given her roly-poly purple VW Bug. Unlocking the door, she murmured, "Been there already, huh?" She glanced skeptically over Wanda's chartreuse linen suit, with its micromini hemline.

Wanda laughed, not insulted in the slightest. "Not on your life. I need a few more years of fun before I settle down. But if you need any help with hints, you just ask your girlfriend Wanda. You're taking a step in the right direction with the makeover, but when you're really ready to step up to the major leagues, you just let me know and I'll see what I can do to help, okay? Good night!"

"Good night," Charlotte replied weakly. She watched Wanda zoom out of the parking lot, her red hair floating behind her. She looked like some ad in a fashion magazine.

Charlotte didn't realize she was still gripping the door handle with a choke hold until long moments later. She opened the door and sat down, then took a quick glance in her mirror. While Wanda's face had still looked porcelain-doll perfect, she herself had lost her lipstick and she had a smudge of pastel high on her right cheek. Where Wanda's red tresses were carefully coifed, her own unruly brown waves were pulled haphazardly in a scrunchy white elastic band, to stay out of her way while she worked. She tugged the band off, watching the locks bounce in front of her eyes. With a deep sigh, she started the car.

Desperate times call for desperate measures.

If she canceled on Jack, she would just be prolonging the agony. She needed to stop these makeover attempts, once and for all. Just one month, she reminded herself. Just one lousy dinner date. She could do this. She *had* to do this.

Well, at least she wasn't going to be under too much pressure. After all, she'd known going in that she would lose the bet, she tried to comfort herself.

Then she decided not to comfort herself. It hurt too much.

4

CHARLOTTE WAS FRANTICALLY dashing around her bedroom when the phone rang.

"Hello?" She tugged her panty hose up to her waist with one hand, tucking the cordless phone between her head and her shoulder with the other.

"So is it true?" Dana asked with no preamble. "You're going on a date with Jack Landor?"

"Bad news travels fast," Charlotte groaned, wondering if Gabe had sent out a press release on it or something. She stalked to her closet. "Yes, it's true. I'm getting dressed, *oof*—" she juggled the phone, buttoning her silk blouse "—as we speak."

"What are you wearing?" Dana's voice held the sharp tone of an interrogator.

"White silk blouse, pinstriped charcoal trousers, low heels, black blazer."

"Are you going on a date or an interview?"

"You're already on my list for putting me in pastels," Charlotte warned, tugging on her pants. "Don't start with me today, Dana. I mean it. I'm on my last nerve."

"Why don't you wear one of your new dresses?" Dana continued, ignoring Charlotte's annoyance.

"Well, A, I wore one of them to work today, B, it's going to be chilly tonight, and C, I don't want to wear anything that screams 'Take me, I'm yours!' to

Jack Landor, who probably has more scantily clad groupies than the Rolling Stones.''

Dana sighed in frustration on the other end of the line. ''If he does have groupies, it's for a darned good reason, Charlotte. The man gives Brad Pitt a run for his money.''

''Did you have something constructive to tell me, or are you just trying to give me an ulcer?'' Charlotte yanked on her blazer impatiently. ''Because if you *don't* have any helpful information to share with me, I'm going to hang up and attempt to drown myself in the bathroom sink.''

''Relax, honey. Breathe,'' Dana said soothingly. ''In through the nose, out through the mouth.''

''Easy for you to say,'' Charlotte replied, trying to take a deep breath. ''You're not having dinner with the most eligible man in America.''

''Well, you must be pretty attracted to him,'' Dana pointed out. ''You said yes to the man, didn't you?''

''Well, yes. But I'm not sure that I would have if Gabe hadn't been hassling me about him.'' Charlotte frowned, then gave her makeup a quick glance in her bedroom mirror. The face there frowned back at her. She'd reapplied her cosmetics carefully, just like the lady at the spa had instructed. It probably worked…it was like looking at the face of a stranger, and it made her uncomfortable. ''I feel like an idiot, Dana. My palms are sweating, and my heart's beating like a jackhammer.''

''Sounds like love,'' Dana suggested in a singsong tone.

''Sounds like terror,'' Charlotte retorted in the same tone. The next time she saw Gabe, she'd strangle him. She wasn't sure how she could prove it, but she was positive this was all his fault!

The doorbell rang, and she jumped, tripping on a

pair of sneakers she'd left lying on the floor. "Oh, no. It's him."

"Remember to take a condom," Dana advised.

Charlotte sighed. "I was thinking more of a cyanide capsule. Good night, Dana." She hung up the phone before Dana could offer any more helpful hints.

Taking a deep breath, she went to the door and opened it slowly as she tried to hold on to her smile.

Jack was waiting, wearing a pair of black chinos and a dark green cable knit sweater that matched his eyes. He looked good, she thought, and her smile curved a little more naturally. "Hi, Jack."

"Hi." He smiled back. "I barely recognized you."

"You're telling me," she said with feeling, grabbing a light jacket and her purse. "I barely recognize myself these days."

When she turned back to face him, he was staring at her strangely. "Why?"

"Why, what?"

"The only time I've seen you, I didn't get a good look at your face," he explained, his smile broadening but his eyes still puzzled. "So it's a surprise to me. But I'm sure you've seen your own face without oatmeal before."

She blushed. *Nothing like starting the evening off feeling stupid!* "Oh, the oatmeal." She laughed self-deprecatingly. "Well, the oatmeal is doing wonders. I'm a completely new person, which is why I have trouble recognizing myself." Somehow that sounded lamer out loud than it did in her head.

"Really?" He gave her a complete once-over. "What did you look like before?"

She smirked at him, putting on her jacket. "I used to be a six-foot-tall Scandinavian, for one thing."

He laughed, and she grinned back weakly. How

long was it going to take him, she wondered, to realize he was going out to dinner with someone completely inept at being a girl?

Oh God, let me survive tonight.

Half an hour later, she was still surviving. Barely.
She had managed to order without embarrassing herself, and there had only been three uncomfortable
pauses. However, she had already managed to knock
over her water twice, and had come perilously close
to setting her menu on fire with the romantic tea-light
candle in the center of the table.

"Sorry," she said, trying to smile. His eyes were
kind, but she felt sure it was a sort of "taking pity
on the handicapped" smile. "I'm not usually this
clumsy."

"At the risk of sounding immodest, I've been
around people who get nervous around me." He
shrugged. "You get used to it."

She frowned. "Well, you *are* gorgeous. I guess I
figured other people must get pretty blasé about that
after a while."

They both blinked at what she said, and she stammered, almost knocking over her third glass of water
that night.

"I'm sorry...that wasn't...oh, God. That sounded
really stupid, didn't it?"

"Actually, that was really cute." He laughed. "I
meant that people usually get nervous about the
money thing. Of course, there is that stupid 'Eligible
Bachelor' thing...."

"I remember reading about that," Charlotte said.
She also remembered Wanda pinning a picture of him
at her desk for about two months.

"Ever since that went into print, I've had women
literally tongue-tied when I wind up going to dinner
with them. Or else chatting their heads off trying to

convince me they're the greatest thing since sliced bread.''

''Ick.'' Charlotte rolled her eyes, laughing. ''No problems here. I am definitely not the greatest thing since sliced bread.''

''I don't know,'' he said, a hint of laughter in his voice. ''It's really easy to talk to you, and you're disarmingly honest, Charlotte.'' His eyes glinted with mischief. ''Or is it Angel? I heard that guy—what was his name?—call you that.''

''Oh,'' she said, feeling a blush heat her cheeks yet again. ''That. My friend Gabe. He just calls me that nickname because he knows it annoys me.''

''Why would being called 'angel' annoy you?''

She sighed. Well, it had been a sort of comedy of errors all night. She was just about getting the hang of being permanently embarrassed, so why not? ''It's stupid, really. When I was little, my dad used to call me Charlie, and Gabe and I used to watch *Charlie's Angels* all the time. Gabe's sister even tried feathering my hair once, with that little flip…you know, like Farrah Fawcett. It was a disaster,'' she said, laughing ruefully at the memory. ''Gabe teased me mercilessly after that. I'm Charlie, the bad hair Angel.''

Jack's smile was warm. ''Well, you don't qualify for bad hair, and you don't really look like a Charlie. The angel part fits well enough, though.''

She smiled, flustered, uncertain of what to do next. It was just a simple compliment, but she wasn't sure how to react. She fell silent, and he waited expectantly. She wished she had anything, absolutely anything, to talk about.

Then she saw *him.*

Gabe sauntered in with a sly smile. He didn't look at her. He was instead riveted on his dining companion for the evening.

The woman was perhaps five-ten with platinum-blond hair and a huge chest that didn't bob when she walked. It was easy to tell, too, in that painted-on dress she was almost wearing. Jeez, Charlotte thought, Gabe had better taste than this, didn't he?

You haven't seen him out with a woman in forever. How are you supposed to know what his taste is? And what do you care?

The woman was draped over Gabe like a shawl. Charlotte felt her blood pressure rise a little.

"Speak of the devil," Jack said. "Isn't that your friend?"

"It would appear to be," she said tightly. "I don't know the woman, though."

"She doesn't seem to be the sort of person one would forget," Jack said with a little cough, looking at the woman skeptically.

Charlotte immediately graced Jack with a radiant smile.

Their dinner arrived as Gabe and the Walking Bust were seated at a table not far from them, behind Jack. Unfortunately, they were in Charlotte's immediate line of vision. She focused on Jack's face and tried not to let her eyes wander to the table where the woman was making playful, teasing gestures with those French-manicured nails of hers. Gabe just smiled as the woman pawed him.

"Something wrong?" Jack asked, frowning with concern.

"Hmm? Oh. Nothing," Charlotte muttered, looking down at her plate. So Gabe was into women who proved there was better living through plastic enhancement. So what? It was a free country.

Gabe leaned forward to catch what his date was saying after they ordered, and Charlotte watched as the woman took an obvious nibble at his ear. Then

Gabe looked directly at Charlotte and gave her a slow, deliberate wink.

Charlotte's breath caught in her throat as something clicked in her mind.

That bum!

It was a setup. She might have guessed! He was showing her the type of woman *The Guide* worked for…the moves, the looks, the surreptitious nibbles. He was rubbing Charlotte's face in the fact that there was no way she could handle this date with Jack. She was outclassed, outmaneuvered and hopelessly out of her league.

She turned to Jack, her heart racing with anger. If Gabe hadn't pushed her into this date, she wouldn't be in this jam in the first place. She'd be damned if he would push her *out* of the same date by making her feel inadequate, by showing up with some hour-glass Kewpie doll!

She took a long, slow sip of her water, letting the icy liquid calm her down a little.

You're a woman. Be a woman.

It was now or never. Charlotte hadn't studied that little paperback for nothing.

She let the straw trail on her lower lip suggestively before putting her drink down. "I love this restaurant," she said, her voice deliberately husky.

Jack's eyes widened, and the forkful of rice he'd begun to eat remained suspended in midair. "Really?"

"Mmm-hmm." She smiled, consciously taking a deep breath high up in her chest. "It's one of my favorite places in Manhattan Beach. It's quiet, it has this great romantic atmosphere, and the food…" She smiled, picking up a forkful of her own risotto and tasting it. The delicate blend of Parmesan and the earthy taste of mushroom blended perfectly with the light, crisp asparagus. She didn't have to play up the moan of satisfaction. ''Well, obviously the food is heavenly.''

He was staring at her as if he'd never seen her before. She beat down the instinct to creep back into her shell. He would react in one of two ways: either he'd think she was absolutely insane, or he'd find it attractive and sensual, just as the book claimed.

His eyes suddenly glowed, a deep, mesmerizing emerald. She'd only seen that sort of look directed at other people, like Dana or Bella, but she knew what it meant. *Full steam ahead.* Now that it was directed at her, she wasn't entirely sure what to do with it. She tried for a sexy smile, and his answering grin was uncomfortably intense.

Gabe's dinner companion broke into the moment with a high-pitched giggle. Charlotte, struggling to keep a grip on whatever she was doing right, reluctantly looked over.

The waiter had delivered a huge salad to Gabe's table. The woman was now feeding forkfuls to Gabe, and he was literally eating it up. The woman's blatant display made Charlotte's subtle little sensual cues look like flirting, Amish-style. She could only imagine what the woman was doing underneath the tablecloth....

Charlotte winced. *Okay. I'm not going to think about* that *again.*

Charlotte forced her focus back to her own table. She glanced down at Jack's plate: poached salmon in a wine sauce. ''Could I have a taste of that?'' she murmured, looking at him hesitantly. ''I've never tried that dish before.'' She knew she ought to be keeping up the sexy act, but in the face of Gabe's competition, she felt herself losing the battle.

Jack smiled, and he picked up a morsel on his fork, holding it out to her.

Her eyes widened. She'd meant could he put it on her plate. She'd never really eaten off another man's fork before, unless you counted Gabe's, which obviously she didn't. The act seemed too intimate, and she started to protest. One glance at Gabe stopped the protest in her throat.

Gabe was staring at Charlotte again, ignoring the lettuce his date was offering. Amazingly enough, he actually had the nerve to look disapproving!

With a slow smile, she leaned forward, taking the salmon neatly off the fork in one small bite. The salmon was incredible, she noted, and she obligingly let out a long sigh.

"God, if I could find that chef, I'd marry him," Charlotte said happily, her eyes half-lidded. *There. Let Gabe disapprove of that!*

Jack leaned over and took her hand, surprising her out of her feelings of triumph. "How about if I just promised to take you here every night?"

She laughed nervously, wondering if she could tug her hand away without seeming too rude. Jack waited a minute, then stroked the back of her hand gently before bringing his own hand back to his side of the table. She suppressed a sigh of relief and made a more concentrated effort to focus on him, rather than the table across the room. She held up her end pretty well, she thought, as they discussed recent movies and books. She concluded that Jack was a nice man, as well as good-looking.

She kept *The Guide* stuff to a minimum, though. Nice or not, Jack definitely made her nervous. When dessert was finally offered, she was more than ready for the date to be over.

"Everything looks so good," Jack said, glancing over at her. "What would you recommend?"

She gave the dessert cart a cursory glance. "The chocolate raspberry decadence sundae," she said immediately. "That's what I'd get, but I'm not really that hungry. I always share it…" She stopped, before she could say *with Gabe*.

He smiled at her, that sexy smile that was beginning to irritate her. "Then we'll share it. Okay?"

She nodded. At this point, she'd agree if he asked to split a hemlock float. She'd had enough dating for one evening.

"Oh Gabe, I shouldn't! Really. Can't you see this dress? I'm supposed to stick to salads!"

Charlotte glanced over at Gabe's table, the dessert cart's next stop. His date was making a lot of noise, attracting most of the patrons' glances and showing off that bionic-woman body of hers. Charlotte rolled her eyes. Jack alone she could have handled, possibly even enjoyed. But Jack and the poster-girl for *The Guide,* both on her first dinner date in years, was more than she could handle.

"Don't worry," Charlotte heard Gabe say over the woman's squealing. "We can split it."

Charlotte saw red.

"Um, Charlotte?" Jack asked tentatively. "Are you okay?"

Charlotte brought her attention back to Jack, immediately feeling guilty. It wasn't his fault that she hadn't dated in so long, or that Gabe was trying to make a point. "I'm sorry, Jack. I've had a lot on my mind lately."

He nodded, and it seemed as if he really understood. "Want to talk about it?"

"Not really."

"You sure?" He smiled and took her hand again,

without any sexy stares or smiles, just friendly. This time, she let him. His hand was warm and comforting. "I'm a good listener."

"You know, I think you would be," she replied, giving his hand a quick squeeze. "But I'm not a great talker, which I guess you probably figured out."

"You were doing fine," he countered. "But I did notice you were kind of distracted. Could you tell me one thing, though?"

She smiled wearily. "Sure. What?"

He glanced over his shoulder, leaned forward and asked quietly, "Why are you so obsessed with that big-chested woman?"

Charlotte's eyes popped wide-open. "Oh, my God."

"Not that she isn't eye-catching, but you've been sending looks over to that table that could skewer things."

Charlotte put her head down on their joined hands, feeling blood rush to her face. "Oh, no…"

He nudged her head up with the back of his hand, forcing her eyes to meet his. "Come on. It's that guy, isn't it? Your friend Gabe."

"No, it's not like that," she muttered, looking desperately in his eyes for understanding. "You see…well, I've known Gabe since I was eight. He's my best friend. But he, along with about all of the male population of Los Angeles, thinks I'm about as sexy as a nature documentary. And being my best friend, he had no real compunction about letting me know that. After all, what are friends for, right?" Her voice broke and she shut up quickly, before she did something even more humiliating. Like crying.

"I've seen some pretty racy nature documentaries," Jack said, causing her to smile and fend off the tears she felt hovering. "And if this guy, or any of the other guys in this city, thinks that you're not absolutely gorgeous, then they're all crazy. You, lady, are one of the prettiest women I've ever seen.''

She snorted. "Pull the other one. I like my legs even."

"I like your legs, too," he said, wiggling his eyebrows and causing her to laugh. "So. What are our friends doing now?" he whispered, leaning over the table, his face set in a melodramatic look of spylike secretiveness.

She sent over a similarly dramatic glance. "She's eating ice cream off of a spoon. He's feeding her," she reported.

"Aw, we can do better than *that*."

She smiled, perfectly at ease with Jack for the first time all night. His answering smile was mischievous, and she chuckled.

Suddenly, she and Jack were putting on a display that would have put *9 1/2 Weeks* to shame. He fed her ice cream, and she devoured it outrageously, darting her tongue out, licking her lips. She fed him spoonfuls, cooing ridiculous names like "Honeybunny" and "Pumpkin Blossom" between bites. It was hysterically funny, especially since no one would expect this kind of behavior from her. Heck, she was surprising herself! It was apparently doing the trick, too... She not only had Gabe's attention, she had drawn the attention of several other tables. It was all she could do not to burst out laughing.

She glanced over to study Gabe's response and was shocked out of her merry state. His date had put aside the spoon and had now scooted her chair closer to Gabe, latching on to his neck like a vampire with her fat pink lips. His eyes were half-closed, like a bored cat's. He barely gave Charlotte a cursory glance as he continued to calmly eat ice cream.

She felt angry, and challenged at the gauntlet Gabe had thrown down. She took one last look at the dish she and Jack had just demolished. The only thing left was the long-stemmed cherry they'd put aside.

"Do you want that cherry?" she asked, glancing at Jack.

"If you want it, it's yours," Jack said, rubbing his stomach and laughing. "I'm going to have a huge stomachache tonight, but it was worth it. I haven't had this much fun in ages!"

"You think that's something," she muttered, picking up the cherry and licking it. "Watch this."

She bit down on the cherry, fiercely ripping it off the stem and devouring it.

"Bravo," Jack said, clapping lightly, but she stopped him with a curt hand motion.

"Not yet," she said, holding the stem. "This is the good part. Watch carefully."

With a quick motion, she sucked the cherry stem in. Her face remained stock-still for a moment, as she moved her tongue in a flurry of hidden activity. Slowly, she smiled, then put her fingers to her lips. With a graceful pull, she produced the cherry stem…only now it was tied in a square knot!

She was gratified by his look of shock. "Party trick," she murmured, shrugging.

Jack's jaw dropped. "I feel like I need a cigarette, and I don't even smoke!"

Applause exploded around her, and Charlotte glanced up.

Two tables of men in business suits were clapping wildly, one man even standing up. "You go, girl!" Wolf whistles emerged from different areas. She even caught several pops of a flashbulb.

Torn between running out of the building and hiding under the table, a gesture that surely would have been misinterpreted, she stood up and curtsied, her face aflame. *The Guide* didn't have a chapter on this one, she reflected. How precisely *did* one look sexy while making a fool of oneself?

Then she looked over at Gabe's table.

Gabe was choking on his ice cream. The busty blonde was hitting him on the back, hard. He only stared at Charlotte, his eyes bulging in shock.

She burst into a radiant smile. *Mess with the bull, and you get the horns, buddy!*

With a flirty little flounce, she turned to Jack. "Well, I guess my work here is done," she murmured, in her best superhero voice. "You ready to go?"

"THAT WAS TOO FUNNY!" Charlotte crowed, feeling drunk as Jack walked her home.

"I think you've pretty much proved your sexiness to the businessmen of South Bay," Jack agreed, ambling next to her. "You sure convinced me."

She sighed. "I can't thank you enough, Jack."

"Anytime." He tugged a lock of her hair gently. "It was my pleasure."

She stopped. "No, really. It...I didn't realize how much it hurt when Gabe said what he did. I know he wasn't trying to be hurtful, but sometimes honesty is worse, you know?"

"He wasn't being honest," Jack said, "he was being mistaken. Why did he say it, anyway?"

She blushed, thinking of the bet. "It's a long story, and it's not really important. I guess he was just trying to make me feel better about being one of the guys. It's not like he really thinks of me as a woman, anyway, so it didn't matter."

"If you're not a woman, what are you?"

What else would you be, a hamster? She smirked

as she remembered Gabe's hooting remark over *The Guide*. "He thinks I'm just like his guy friends. We watch football together, we watch movies together. He's attempted to teach me to surf, but I'm hopeless," she explained, starting to walk again. "He was with me when my father died. I was with him when he got his MBA. He's my best friend, Jack. He wouldn't lie to me."

"Maybe he just can't handle the truth," Jack mused.

"What truth can't he handle?" she muttered, frowning and pulling a flower off of a nearby jasmine bush.

Jack smiled. "Why don't you keep thinking about it, and let me know what you come up with."

Within minutes, they were at their street. Stopping in front of the trellis over the gate to her walkway, she paused, wondering what to do next. She liked Jack, but she didn't want to invite him in. Well, she did sort of want to invite him in, but only to talk, and from the way their conversation was running, they'd only talk about Gabe. Even for a casual date, that seemed tacky.

"Well, I guess this is my stop," she said, shifting her weight nervously from foot to foot. "Thanks for taking me out tonight, Jack."

"We'll have to do it again sometime," he said, his grin like summer lightning. "Um...this is usually the 'good-night kiss' part."

She smiled weakly, taking a half step back. "Would you believe I don't kiss on the first date?"

"Would you believe that's the first time outside of a movie I've heard that?" He laughed. He didn't come any closer, though. "I like you, Charlotte Taylor."

She grinned back, relieved. "I like you, too, Jack Landor."

"Say, I have an idea. What are you doing Saturday?"

She rolled her eyes. "A whole lot of nothing. Why?"

"There's this big party, formal dress thing over in Century City. It'll probably be a crashing bore, but I think I'd have a lot more fun if you were there. Will you come with me?"

Charlotte felt her stomach constrict. "Formal dress? As in, really fancy?"

He nodded, and his eyes were pleading. "I don't know a lot of girls out here…I'm out from New York for only a couple of months. It would be a huge favor to me if you'd come. Please?"

She sighed. He'd been such a great sport about the dinner. It seemed to be the least she could do. "All right, Jack. You're on."

"Super." He gave her a broad grin. "I'll pick you up Saturday at seven. See you then." He kissed her cheek quickly, then whistled his way down to his front gate.

She turned to her own walkway, stepping up to her front door and unlocking it. She walked into her empty house, shutting the door behind her.

Jack was warm, funny, gentle and nice. He was, just as most magazines claimed, everything a woman would want in a man. So why didn't her heart race when he talked to her? Why wasn't she getting all gooey and weak in the knees when he flashed that gorgeous smile? Most of all, why hadn't she invited that sun-god bod of his up to her place, so she could break her several-year streak of celibacy?

Maybe there was something wrong with her.

She was tired, and confused, the little rush of triumph she'd had at the restaurant dissipating. She needed to talk this out, make sense of it somehow.

Not really thinking, she walked over to her room. Flopping on her bed, she picked up the phone and dialed it blindly, completely by reflex.

"Hello?" she heard Gabe's voice say darkly over the crackle of a cellular phone.

She froze. She'd called Gabe, of course, ready to ask him to come over because she needed to talk.

But what was she going to say? That it hurt to hear the truth from him? That she'd made a fool of herself tonight all because of him? That she couldn't ask Jack in, and she didn't know why? What would Gabe think? What would he say?

After a few seconds, he gave an irritated huff and hung up. Listening to the dial tone, she buried her face in her pillow. To her surprise, she felt a tear trickle hotly down her cheek.

Okay, maybe this bet had gone too far. She would talk to him tomorrow, and somehow clear this all up. Having all the men in the world strewn at her feet was pointless if she lost her best friend over it.

5

GABE SAT AT HIS DESK the following morning, staring at his computer. He'd been to two meetings, dictated several memos and reports, and plowed through half a dozen licensing proposals for Lone Shark Licensing dealers. Unfortunately, he hadn't really been paying attention to any of them.

He had been up way too late the night before, but at least he had finally gotten a grip on the situation—and gotten even with Charlotte in the process. It was her fault he was sandy-eyed and unable to focus this morning, he thought. A little revenge was not just appropriate, it was mandatory.

When he'd left the restaurant, his date in tow, he was mad enough to spit nails. The plan had been to show Charlotte just how badly these *Guide* women could behave, how patently obvious their tactics could be, and Terri had filled that teaching position perfectly. What he had not expected was that Charlotte would not only miss the point, but eclipse even Terri's blatant performance. He was so incensed, he'd planned on dropping Terri off, heading to Charlotte's house and having it out with her then and there. When it suddenly occurred to him that Charlotte might not be alone, he all but stuffed Terri in a cab.

Before he could tear off to Charlotte's house, the businessmen who had been having their dinner meeting at the restaurant burst out raucously. With a stroke of luck, he managed to buy a roll of film from one of the men who had taken her picture.

By that point, he had gotten under control. Charlotte wasn't going to do anything with Jack...she wasn't that type of woman, which was fortunate for Jack's chances of survival. Charlotte had acted that way to take revenge on him. She'd turned the tables on him, and done it well. She'd expect him to do the same...and with pictures, he thought, he would do just that.

Taking the film to a one-hour Photomat had managed to produce one dark but distinct picture of Charlotte in the process of devouring that infamous cherry. He could have simply embarrassed her with it. The problem was, she was a master at revenge...like the time she had created a picture of him buck-naked except for an artfully placed party hat, and printed it on his surprise birthday invitations.

He smiled grimly. When it came to bets, he and Charlotte never did anything simply. Sometime in the next few hours, she'd get a nice little volley back in retaliation for her performance last night.

Frankly, her performance had shaken him badly.

He wished he could say it was anger, but he knew better. Just thinking of the episode made his blood heat, even now.

He got up to open his window, hoping that a cool breeze from the ocean would lower his temperature. He could only enjoy it for a second before his door flew open.

"What the hell is this?"

Gabe smiled out the window. He knew that irate female voice well. "Hi, Charlotte. What brings you here?"

He turned to see her, hazel eyes flashing with rage. She was wearing an ice-blue sweater set with a miniskirt that showed off her long legs like an art display. His temperature inched up another notch. Before anything else could inch up, he grabbed the printout she held, focusing on it as if it were the most important document in the world.

"It appears to be a picture of you eating...what's that? A cherry?" He suppressed a grin.

"No," she said, her voice hard enough to shape diamonds. "What I mean is, how did this get sent to *my* computer department?"

He blinked, feigning innocence. "I don't know what you're talking about."

"Oh, don't you?" She advanced on him, the look in her eyes murderous. "Then why is it that Ryan, our poker buddy and my co-worker, popped this into *your* company Web site?"

Gabe bit his tongue. He and Ryan had pulled practical jokes on Charlotte in the past, since Ryan's presence at Howes Design made sneaking things into her office or car that much easier. When Gabe had called Ryan last night, Ryan had jumped at the idea. It was going to be one of Gabe's best pranks yet. "I can't imagine," he said, struggling with a straight face.

"I can!" she yelped, poking him hard in the chest. "Everybody knows that Gabe Donofrio picks the photo for that asinine Lone Shark Babe of the Week page and posts it on the Internet. How dare you take my picture and put it there!"

He chuckled and dodged a hard punch in the stomach. "Now, now, calm down. I got the point across. Besides, it couldn't have been on for more than an hour or so."

"It was on all night!"

His laughter stopped dead. All night? What happened? "I told Ryan about this last night, true," he said sharply. "He told me he didn't come into the office until ten at the earliest, and it's only eleven-thirty.''

''Yeah, well, he thought this was so amusing that it wouldn't wait until morning,'' she said, her voice dripping with bitterness. ''And since everyone *knows* the new girl gets posted on Thursday, your little prank has been open season for any acne-covered horndog who regularly checks your Web site *since midnight last night.*''

He blanched. This had not been his plan at all. ''He didn't put your name on it, did he?''

''No, and it's the only reason he's still alive. If Wanda hadn't warned me, God knows how many people would have seen it by now. Our Web site support people say we've been getting hits like crazy, all wanting to know who the mysterious 'cherry girl' is. Can you believe this?''

''Oh, God.'' Gabe rubbed his hands over his face. ''You've got to believe me…it wasn't supposed to happen this way. I thought maybe you'd get ribbed at work, but…''

Gabe's executive assistant walked in. ''Um, boss?''

Gabe frowned, wishing Charlotte had shut the door before she exploded. ''Yes, Jake, what is it?''

Jake's eyes never left Charlotte's legs. ''Um…did you finish going over those memos I typed up for you?''

Gabe walked over to his desk, thankful that it gave him time to try to compose his apology. As he started to sift through the piles of papers, the younger man walked up to Charlotte. ''Hi there. I'm Jake. I saw you on the Web site.''

''Did you?'' She sent a poisonous glance over to Gabe. Gabe quickly shifted his focus back to his desktop.

"Yeah, and I was wondering if maybe you'd be interested in dinner sometime. Or maybe a movie?"

"You know, Jake—" Gabe's voice cut through Jake's invitation like steel "—I can't find them right now, and I'm obviously in the middle of something. I'll get them to you later."

Jake looked ready to continue his pursuit, but a hard glare from Gabe sent him packing. "Oh. Sorry, boss."

Gabe escorted him to the door. Before Gabe could shut it, however, three other men walked up to him, papers in hand. "Is she in there?" one asked quietly, trying to glance around Gabe's chest.

"What do you guys want?" Gabe said shortly.

They shifted their feet, ignoring him even as they thrust documents at him. "We just thought you might have time to look these over."

Gabe took a quick look at one of the sheets. "Dammit, Bill, this is a memo you sent me last *month.*"

Bill smiled sheepishly. "Cut me some slack, Gabe. I needed an excuse to get in here. Is that woman hot, or what?"

Hot? Other men were calling his Charlotte *hot?*

Gabe gritted his teeth, taking a deep breath for patience. "I'm in a closed-door meeting for the next half hour. I'll talk with you later." Without another word, he shut the door in their faces, and locked it.

He turned back to Charlotte. She was still on her feet, eyes blazing. He deserved it. It had moved beyond the playful prank that was so characteristic of their friendship. She had every right to be angry.

But it wasn't the anger that worried him. In all their years of playful warfare, in all their competitions and rough times, he'd never seen this look of pain on her face.

"Charlotte, I'm sorry," he said, knowing that the

words did little and would not erase the anguish he was seeing. "I swear, I didn't mean it to work out this way. It was just a joke. You know how we are, Charlotte. It was just…"

"Tell me something, will you?" Her voice was low and uneven. "How is it an intelligent man like yourself can be so completely clueless when it comes to women?"

"What do you mean?"

"Oh, right, I forgot…I'm not really a woman, not to you." Her voice was as bitter as coffee grounds. "I'm just good old Charlie, one of the guys. Fine for providing food, hanging out with, making fun of."

"You make fun of me just as much as I make fun of you," he argued, wishing she'd turn around.

"Oh, right. Add 'gives as good as she gets' to that list. Did it ever occur to you that just once, I'd like to be able to take it easy? I know I haven't had much practice, but I'd like to try being girly and sensitive. I'd even like to cry once in a while. Did you ever think that what you were saying and doing was hurting me?"

That punctured him. "God, Charlotte. You know I never want to hurt you."

She finally turned around, and her eyes were swimming in unshed tears. "Then why are you?"

"Charlotte," he breathed. He was over at her side in an instant. "Angel, I'm sorry, I'm so sorry." He tugged her up out of the chair and into his arms. "I mean it. I didn't know that dumb prank was going to hurt you like this, I'm sorry."

She cried on his shoulder for a minute, delicate, soft little sobs that ripped his heart apart. He hadn't known. Why hadn't he known?

Because she was right. Until recently, he *had* only seen her as one of the guys. She was so strong, so ready to go head-to-head with him at the drop of a hat. It never occurred to him that she wouldn't say anything until the hurt was so bad she was drowning in it. He was so intent on keeping his "perfect life" intact that he'd failed to see what she was going through. He was such an idiot!

"I'm sorry, Gabe. Last night, then the Web site… I guess it was the last straw." She pulled back, and her eyes were huge and liquid, the hazel color luminescent. "I guess I don't really have the right to be angry at you for speaking your mind. But I have to say this. It's hard to hear from your best friend that you're not pretty, not feminine, that you're never going to get married…."

"Hey, wait a minute," he interrupted, giving her a gentle shake. "I never said anything like that!"

She tilted her head to the side, a sad smile on her face. "Not precisely, but then, did you need to spell it out? I've known you for forever. I knew what you were trying to say." She pushed out of his arms, walking over to the window as she wiped her eyes with the backs of her hands. "Heck. It's impossible to disagree with you. I mean, look at me. What would a man want with someone like me?"

"Are you kidding? Charlotte, you have plenty to offer a man." He leaped to her defense, trying to undo some of the damage he'd caused. "You're smart, and sexy, and funny. You just don't see it in yourself."

"Not you, too," she said, hiccuping. "I thought you of all people would agree with me."

If possible, he felt even lower. "You know I'm on your side, Charlotte."

"You haven't been. Not since this stupid bet got started." She turned on him, her eyes large and luminous. "Do you know why I stuck with it? Because if I lose, your sister and Dana promised they'll finally get off my back and let me live my life, my way. It's the easiest solution. Or at least, it seemed like it was...until you decided to go to war.''

''Charlotte, please. I already feel so low, I could walk under a rattlesnake. Wearing a top hat.'' Gabe rubbed a tear off her cheek. ''I was just being selfish. I was...'' He paused, taking a deep breath, and admitted to Charlotte what he'd never admit in front of anybody else...not his family, not the Hoodlums, not anyone. ''I was afraid. I was scared you'd change into one of those superficial, man-crazy *Guide* girls. And I was afraid I'd lose the best friend I have. How lame is that, right?''

She sent him a watery smile. ''Actually, I kind of know how you feel. I tried calling you last night. I chickened out, because I didn't know how to talk to you about all of this.''

He stuck out his hand. ''Let's make a pact. No matter what happens, we stay best friends. That means we can talk to each other about anything, and whatever else is going on in our lives, we're there for each other. Deal?''

She shook his hand. ''Deal,'' she said, then threw her arms around him. ''Let's not go through this again.''

He returned the hug fiercely, crushing her to him. ''We won't. I'm not going to risk losing you again, angel.''

They probably didn't have to hug quite that long, but one minute seemed to stretch into another, and neither were in any hurry to leave the comfort of the other. She felt compact, fitting snugly against his body. He stroked the back of her head, feeling the silky softness of her hair beneath his fingers, and heard her sigh. He looked down, and she looked up.

Her cheeks were flushed, and her eyes were wide and clear, and looking up at him with that tenderness that he hadn't seen in way too long.

Any woman who looks at you like that deserves to be good and kissed, Gabe.

Damn fine idea, he thought. Finally, his conscience had decided to help out, instead of being such a pill all the time. He leaned down, close, his eyes never leaving hers.

Just a breath away from her lips, he stopped.

Wait a second. What am I doing?

He jerked away as if she were an electrified fence. He put a few crucial feet of space between them, then stared at her. He could feel his heart pounding in his chest like a jackhammer, and noticed that her eyes were huge, almost wary.

"Well. I'm glad we got that all straightened out," he said gruffly.

"Oh. Me, too." Charlotte still stared at him.

"So." He cleared his throat. Boy, that was a close one. What had he been thinking? "I've got an idea of how I can make it up to you."

She sighed. "This ought to be humorous."

"It's my fault you're stuck in this bet. The logical conclusion would be that it's now my responsibility to help you out of it."

"Gabe," Charlotte said in a skeptical tone, "I think you've helped enough, don't you?"

"I didn't know what was going on," he argued. "The problem is, you need to put on a really good show, get a little more comfortable around guys."

"Oh, come on," she said, laughing. "I've been hanging out with the Hoodlums since I could drive. Now you think the problem is I'm awkward around men?"

"But you *are* awkward…when you're being a

woman.'' He looked her over. ''I've got it. We'll do a trial run. Are you busy tonight?''

''You're kidding, right?'' She narrowed her eyes at him, then shrugged. ''Nope. No dates tonight, and what a shock that is. But it is a designated date night. Dana will probably drop by and drag me somewhere. I hope she doesn't bring her husband with her. How awkward would *that* be?''

''Can you figure a way out of it, and meet me at Sharkey's, around seven?''

''Sure.''

''And dress up.''

Her eyes widened. ''Huh?''

''Just trust me,'' he said, nodding. ''With any luck, it'll make this bet business a snap.''

''You're lucky I'm your best friend, because no sane woman would put up with you,'' she answered, then nodded. ''Seven at Sharkey's. Got it.''

THE PROBLEM WAS, this had seemed like a good idea in theory. Now, looking at it, it occurred to Gabe that this whole plan would have worked a lot better if the guys hadn't taken their jobs so *seriously*.

''Gabe, this is ridiculous,'' Charlotte said, laughing.

''I think Gabe had a spectacular idea,'' Sean said, throwing an arm around her shoulders. ''If you want to learn to catch a guy, you gotta go to the source.''

''Nobody said anything about catching guys,'' Gabe said sharply. ''I just said she needed to be more comfortable around them when she's dressed up.''

And dressed up she was. She looked sharp in a dark lavender dress, similar to the pink one he'd first seen on her when this whole mess started. She was wearing heels again, too. He scrupulously avoided staring at her legs. Or her chest. Or her face, really. He'd pretty much resigned himself to talking to the top of her head.

But the other guys had no such problems.

"Hey, pretty lady," Mike said, beaming his best come-on smile at her. "Come here often?"

"Mike, we were just here last Monday night, remember? Catching the game?"

Mike frowned, nonplussed. "Oh. Right." He brightened, and tried the smile again. "But you didn't look like *this,* gorgeous."

"Gabe, this is insane." She walked over to where he was standing. He noticed the guys riveted to the gentle sway of her hips, and had to stop himself from glaring at them. "It's not like they're really *men.* They're just the Hoodlums."

"I resent that," Sean piped up.

"Yeah, just give us a try, baby," Ryan said, wiggling his eyebrows. "We'll be *plenty* enough love for you, hot stuff."

"Hot stuff? Gorgeous? What, do you guys get handed a manual in high school or something?"

"Gabe," Sean whined. "She's not taking this *seriously.*"

"How can I?" Charlotte laughed. She was wearing a darker lipstick, too, and her eyes seemed even larger in the dim light. Whatever she was doing with makeup was working, big time. "You guys keep clowning around."

"Just pretend you're at some big party or something," Gabe said, trying his best to be focused. He'd promised her he'd get her out of the mess he'd landed her in. He meant it. If he had to help her become the girliest woman on the face of the planet, then he'd do it. "No matter what the guys say, just keep smiling, but throw attitude at them."

"What kind of attitude?" Charlotte asked, bewildered.

"Like they're bugs." He smiled. Teaching her to be girly didn't mean she had to be a pushover, however. He wasn't about to teach her how to catch a guy. "Like you're the most beautiful woman alive, and they're wasting your time. Like they're insane to even *dream* they've got a chance at you."

"Hey, Gabe, no fair," Mike said, frowning. "I get treated like that by every other woman I meet. You're ruining all my fun here."

Charlotte smiled wickedly, slowly getting the idea. "You mean, treat them like dirt, and they'll revere me as a goddess?"

"It's a trade secret, but yup, that's it." Gabe smiled back, savoring the look on her face. This was going to be good.

She sashayed back to the bar stool she'd been sitting on. Gabe couldn't help but be riveted this time, either…the sassy little swing in her hips was mesmerizing.

Mike stepped up to the plate again. "Hey, pretty lady…"

Her eyes were wide and sexy, but her voice was coolly amused. "This—" she gestured down the length of her body "—is not for you." She pointed at him, then smiled and looked away.

Mike goggled. Ryan laughed and nudged him aside. "Excuse me, miss, do you have thirty-five cents?" He grinned. "My mother told me to call her when I fell in love."

Charlotte reached into her purse and produced three quarters. "Here. After you reach her, try calling somebody who cares."

"Ooh, she's good," Sean said as Ryan good-naturedly grumbled and stepped back. "Here's a better one. Are you tired? Because you've been running through my mind all night long.''

Charlotte tried to look bored, but the humor glinted through her eyes. Finally, she broke down and laughed. "Okay. You win. You get one dance.''

Sean broke into a huge grin, leading her off to the dance floor. "Works every time,'' he called over his shoulder, before pushing his way through the shimmying crowd.

Gabe watched as Charlotte moved, noticing that several pairs of male eyes were watching her with predatory awareness.

He prayed he didn't have the same look on his own face.

He didn't want to be attracted to her. He didn't want to change what they had. All this time, they'd been friends. At first, he could still superimpose the image of her as a bratty eight-year-old over her. When that didn't work, he focused on her grubby jeans and oversize sweatshirts.

Frankly, he'd never *let* himself see Charlotte as a woman before. Now he didn't have much choice. The proof of her transformation hit him in the face like a slap.

He watched as she laughed at some joke Sean was making. She looked incredible. She was happy, vibrant, so alive she almost shimmered with it.

He wanted her.

Want all you want, his conscience chimed in, *but hands off. She's a friend, remember?*

He hated to admit it, but his conscience was right. It was the cornerstone of his life. Women come and women go, but friends are for life. After their massive fight this afternoon, he had gotten a taste of just how painful it could be if he lost his friendship with Charlotte. It might be bad if he couldn't spend as much time with her because she got married. It would be a comparative hell, however, if he couldn't see her ever again.

He was the first to admit that his relationships didn't last long, and those that had lasted a long time had ended with harsh words and no further contact. He wasn't about to risk that with Charlotte. If he did get physical with Charlotte, it would be a relationship. He wasn't so dumb that he didn't realize that.

So he wouldn't get physical with her. He'd just be her friend, and that was that.

The song finished, and Sean led Charlotte away by one hand, grinning like a fool. Before they could make it to the side of the floor, another man stepped in front of Charlotte, stopping her.

Gabe shot to his feet.

Charlotte's eyes widened as the man yelled something to her over the fast tempo of the next song. She glanced nervously at Sean, who shrugged. She bit her lower lip, then shrugged, herself, and accompanied the man back out on the dance floor.

Sean walked over to Gabe, whose mouth had dropped open. "Can you believe that? One dance, and that guy just sneaks in and steals Charlotte out from under me."

Gabe ignored the disturbing thought that phrase provoked. "What were you thinking?" he yelled instead. "She's off with a perfect stranger!"

"So?" Sean shrugged. "She seems to be holding her own. That was the point of this whole exercise, wasn't it?"

Gabe saw the man try to dance a little too close to Charlotte, presumably under the pretext of whispering something to her. Gabe started to stride toward the floor with the intention of beating the man senseless.

"Whoa, whoa!" Sean grabbed him. "Easy, fella. She's okay."

Gabe growled but noticed that Charlotte firmly nudged the man away from her, shaking her head. She wore the same expression that she'd sent to Mike earlier. *This is not for you,* he saw her mouth to the man, frowning.

His breathing eased.

"You know," Sean said perceptively, "if you're not going to sell something, don't put it in the window."

"What the hell is that supposed to mean?" Gabe said, too intent on keeping track of Charlotte to really pay attention to his friend's inscrutable words.

Sean gave him a gentle shove. "It means she looks beautiful, man. Leave her alone."

"I am leaving her alone," Gabe growled.

"Obviously."

Charlotte walked back to the group with her dance partner following her like a puppy. She had a small smile on her face. She turned. "Thanks for the dance."

"Can I have your number?" the man asked eagerly.

She thought about it for a minute. "No."

"Why not?"

"You heard her, buddy," Gabe said, glowering at him as he put an arm around Charlotte's shoulders. "Back off."

"All right, all right. Jeez." The man frowned at Gabe, then sent one last hopeful smile at Charlotte. "I loved your picture on the Web site. I can't wait to tell the guys I danced with the Lone Shark Babe of the Week."

Charlotte's eyes widened as the man walked away.

"It was a great picture, you've got to admit," Ryan said, chuckling at her surprise.

She arched an eyebrow at him, pinning him to the seat with a glare. "Really. And that was what prompted you to post it for twelve hours."

Ryan smirked, unrepentant. "Got a good number of hits, too. The mystery thing really got a lot of guys going. Besides, I think they were starting to get tired of the models we were using."

"Oh, I'm sure." Charlotte's glare intensified.

"No, really. Well, they weren't complaining. A babe is still a babe." Ryan grabbed a handful of peanuts and shrugged. "But most of the babes we had on the site were these 'hand me the cocoa butter' babes that only exist on mythical tropical islands. No average guy is going to run into her in a supermarket."

"So what's your point?" Charlotte asked skeptically. "I'm a 'pass the frozen peas' babe?"

"The point is, you're obviously in real life…you're gorgeous, but you're also available. And that's kind of a turn-on." He grinned lasciviously. "That thing with your tongue was pretty hot, too. I kept a copy of the photo for myself."

She covered her face with her hands. "Oh, God…"

"Hey, can I get a few copies?" Sean inquired. "A couple of guys down at the surf shop wanted to see her, but she got taken off the site too soon."

"No, you can't," Charlotte and Gabe said at the same time.

"All right, all right." Sean looked pained. "Sheesh."

Charlotte took a quick glance at her watch and groaned. "I've got to go, fellas. Thanks for the… education."

The guys put up a chorus of complaints. "It's still

early," Sean pleaded, smiling. "What, you got an early date tomorrow or something?"

"Two, actually," she said, causing Gabe's eyes to narrow. "The first being a spa date with Dana, starting with an early-morning jog. And since it's Dana, that means *really* early."

"What's the other one?"

"You won't believe it," Charlotte said. "There's this big party at the Century Plaza. Big formal dress thing. If he weren't in such a jam for a date, I'd say no. I mean, you know I'm not comfortable at those kind of things. If I can just get through it without making a fool of myself, I'll be happy." She stared pointedly at Ryan. "*Especially* after the Web site thing."

Ryan had the grace to look embarrassed. Gabe felt an aftershock of the guilt he'd been hit with that afternoon.

She nodded with satisfaction. "Well, I'm glad we both learned a lesson tonight," she said, smiling. "I'll see you guys later."

"I'll walk you to your car," Gabe said.

"It's not that far...."

"I'm coming with you," he said insistently.

"Don't try to get her number," Mike warned, grinning. ":Trust me. She's tough!"

They left amid a barrage of catcalls and loud commentary from the Hoodlums. Charlotte just smiled. Gabe didn't.

"Thanks for the help, Gabe," Charlotte said, unlocking Jellybean. "I know this can't be easy for you."

He grimaced. "What can't be?"

"The fact that you're trying to help me stick with this bet." She shrugged. "I might have to pay you that thousand in installments...."

"Don't be an idiot," he said, rolling his eyes. "We'll work out something."

She nodded with a thankful smile, then shivered.

"Here," he said, taking off the light jacket he was wearing and throwing it over her shoulders. "You'll catch cold."

"How did I get lucky enough to get a best friend like you?" She gave him a quick hug.

He told his arms not to go around her, but they wouldn't listen.

"Good night," she said casually, obviously not having any of the problems he was having. She got in her car.

"Good night," he replied, and watched her drive out of the parking lot.

He walked back in, frowning.

"Where's your jacket?" Sean asked, glancing at him.

"Charlotte was cold."

"She ought to be," Mike joked. "That was not much of a dress she was wearing. But what she *was* wearing," he said, rolling his eyes heavenward, "was *choice.*"

"So how'd we do?" Ryan asked. "Is she now a kick-butt, man-eating machine?"

"I wouldn't go that far, but I guess we helped," Gabe replied. She certainly looked comfortable enough when she was dancing with that guy. "She's not looking forward to that party tomorrow, though. I wish there were some way we could help her out. That thing with the Web site really got to her." And he'd be damned if he saw her go through that much pain ever again.

"Wait a second…" Ryan said. "There might be a way. She said Century Plaza, right?"

"Right," Gabe said hesitantly. "So?"

"So," Ryan said, "that means it's the Sheffield party."

"Again, so?"

"*So*, I know the printer who makes all the Sheffield invitations," Ryan said, and grinned expectantly.

It took Gabe a second for Ryan's words to sink in. When they did, a matching grin spread across his face.

"Break out your tuxes, boys," he said, snickering and feeling better for the first time that night. "Looks like we've got a party to crash."

6

"I DIDN'T KNOW, CHARLOTTE. I swear to God, I had no idea."

Charlotte didn't even look up from her glass of champagne. "And I still believe you, Jack. Really. Just let it go."

He studied her for a moment, his emerald eyes lighting with warmth. "I can't believe you're being so calm about this. If I were you, I'd be dumping that glass of champagne all over me."

Charlotte grinned. "Now that I've made sense out of that sentence, it really isn't as bad as all that, Jack."

"There must be five hundred people out there," Jack countered, "and they're all staring at *you*. But that's not a big deal?"

She thought about it a second. "Well, it's not your fault I decided to wear red. And it's not your fault that you didn't remember that the Sheffield Ball is also called Los Angeles' Black and White Ball because…"

"Everybody wears black and white," Jack said, shaking his head. "Why didn't anybody tell me?"

"I think it was on the invitation that you didn't really read," Charlotte suggested. "Okay, so maybe it was your fault, a little. And it is definitely your fault that I'm sitting under a spotlight at the head table, but…"

Jack groaned and put his head down on his hands.

Charlotte laughed. "Okay. Feel guilty. You deserve it."

"I owe you for this one, Charlotte."

She shrugged again. "Jack, after what I've been through this week, this is nothing."

When she had walked in with Jack, she had seen the sea of stark, unbroken black and white, and frozen. Five hundred pairs of eyes had snapped on her, staring as if she'd just emerged from a spaceship. It was strangely reminiscent of her old nightmare of showing up for a big class design review in her ratty old underwear. Her initial reaction had been to turn, run back out the doors, steal Jack's keys from the valet and make an escape. But she hadn't. Instead, she kept her chin up, her eyes wide and her smile bright. Even if she had a blush that matched her deep red dress, she wouldn't let them see otherwise how humiliating the experience was.

The fact was, she loved the dress, and it was the first time in her life she could actually say that. She'd put up with the pastel confections that Derek, her ex-boyfriend, had created, and the similarly frail summer dresses that Dana had fobbed off on her. But this, a simple, minimal sheath in a dark burgundy, had practically yelled "Charlotte!" when she stepped into the store. She'd turned down all the peaches and pale pinks that Dana had suggested, and when she tried her dress on, even Dana and the saleswoman had to admit it was fantastic. It fit her like a glove, and she felt like a queen in it.

She remembered that every time she saw someone stare at her with a look of amusement, or worse, contempt. She looked pretty good in her red dress. Pretty *darned* good. So if everybody else was wearing black and white, so what?

She'd been caked in mud in front of the most eligible bachelor in America. She'd practically smeared whipped cream all over herself in a public restaurant. She was the pinup of the week on a national Web site. And she had made grown men weep at a nearby sports bar. Compared to all that, wearing red in front of a bunch of L.A. socialites was a cakewalk!

The funny thing was, she really needed to thank Gabe for his part in her new confidence, even if he didn't realize that he had helped her. If he hadn't pushed her, she never would have realized how much she could take…or how much she had to give. She wasn't sure how it happened, but somehow a lot of things she used to view as ''terrifying'' were suddenly trivial. She wasn't going to die of embarrassment. In fact, she wasn't even going to *see* most of these people again. The people she really cared about thought she was fine. More than that. They thought she was beautiful.

She was pretty sure Gabe thought she was, at least.

She frowned, remembering that strange moment in his office. He'd leaned so close she could practically feel currents of energy running off of him. For a brief, crazed moment, she thought he might have kissed her.

Not that that was what she wanted. She'd known for years that Gabe was handsome. If anything, he was *too* handsome. Men like that were never interested in women like her, so it hadn't occurred to her to see him as anything but a friend. But for a brief moment, hadn't she hoped…

No. That wasn't going to happen. The things that *were* happening to her were strange enough.

''That's quite a dress,'' a woman walking past their table said, her voice catty.

''Thanks. I love it,'' Charlotte said easily. ''The

way I see it, red stands out so much better against black and white, don't you think?''

''I certainly think so,'' the woman's date agreed, giving Charlotte a serious once-over and leering. Charlotte winked at him. The woman gasped in shock before hurrying her date away, hissing at him as they left.

Charlotte looked at Jack, who was goggling at her. ''What?'' she asked, smoothing her hair.

''Who are you, and what have you done with Charlotte Taylor?''

She chuckled. ''I know. It's like the invasion of the pod people, only this time with a sense of humor.''

Jack shook his head. ''You amaze me, Charlotte. You don't seem like the girl I had dinner with the other night at all.''

She sobered slightly, considering his words. ''Is that a bad thing?''

''No,'' he said quickly. ''It's just…well, it's like somebody found your volume control and turned it all the way up.''

She shot him a skeptical glance. ''And that's supposed to be better?''

He grinned and gently stroked his fingertip along her jawline. ''It is when you've been whispering for years, beautiful.''

She smiled again. If this kept up, her cheek muscles were going to be cramping. But she couldn't help herself.

''I need to go mingle…there are some big fund-raisers here tonight,'' Jack said. ''Want to come with me?''

''Nah,'' she said. ''I've talked to more people tonight than I have in years. I thought I'd people-watch a little bit, maybe sit out on the sidelines.''

"Okay, pretty girl," Jack said. "Give me half an hour and I'll take you home."

"Deal."

He gave her a quick peck on the cheek, then headed out toward the milling guests. They clumped around him like iron filings on a magnet. He disappeared into the crowd.

She stood up and started walking toward one of the freestanding bar setups, eager to get a glass of ice-cold water. He was a nice guy, that Jack. After her years of not dating at all, he was an incredibly good "training wheels" date. The only person who had been more sweet and supportive than he was...

She blinked. Was Gabe, now that she thought about it. But Gabe was just a friend, so naturally he didn't count.

There it was again, that flash from Gabe's office.

No, Charlotte. He doesn't count.

A honey-blond woman stopped her, looking her over. "Great dress," she said. Her tone was genuine, with none of the sarcasm or venom of the woman Charlotte had spoken with earlier.

"Thanks," Charlotte said, smiling. "I have to admit, though, I didn't know about the black-and-white dress code thing."

"Really?" The woman smiled back, and her voice was warm. Charlotte thought she recognized her from a movie she'd seen. "I was sitting at my table envying the hell out of you, ready to rip into my agent for not thinking of trying a red dress last year. You're getting great buzz tonight, so I figured you must be an actress."

"No," Charlotte hastily explained. "I'm a designer."

"That explains it," the woman said, snapping her

fingers. "It's written all over you. Have I seen your fall collection?"

It took Charlotte a minute to figure out what she was asking. Then she quickly shook her head. "Oh, no. I'm not that kind of designer. I'm a graphic designer. I haven't done fashion stuff in years."

"You might want to rethink that. That dress suits you perfectly…it's simple yet smashing. Sort of Grace Kelly does Versace."

Charlotte glanced down at her dress, grinning foolishly. "You know, I was thinking more Audrey Hepburn does Vera Wang."

"Better!" The woman reached inside her purse and handed Charlotte a card. "That does it. If you're up for it, I'd love to have you work with me on my dress for the Oscars next year. I'm always looking for a killer stylist. I have a good feeling about you."

A stylist? *Her?* "Um, sure. I mean, I'll think about it."

The woman smiled brilliantly before moving back into the crowd.

Okay, now this would be the part where I wake up.

But Charlotte didn't wake up. She was still standing there, in her off-the-rack red dress, holding the business card of one of the most successful actresses in Hollywood.

Charlotte felt like singing. She was queen of the world. She was invincible. She was a cross between Marilyn Monroe and Mighty Mouse. Oh, if only the Hoodlums could see her now!

She heard the steady rumbling of conversation slow, then grind to a halt. Curious, she looked toward the doorway.

Speak of the devil.

The Hoodlums were framed in the large doorway, standing resplendent. Gabe, Ryan, Mike and Sean posed like *GQ* sentinels, completely indifferent to the stir they were creating.

It was strange enough to see her poker crew at a Sheffield party, much less their Black and White Ball. But as she glanced over their formal attire, she noticed that something was missing.

Namely, their pants.

They were all wearing brilliant white shirts and black tuxedo jackets. But from the waist down, they wore long, loose-fitting surfer shorts in every color under the sun, paired with black suede high-topped sneakers. Both the shorts and the sneakers displayed a large logo…the distinctive shark with sunglasses that Charlotte herself had designed for Gabe's sportswear company!

In unison, the Hoodlums removed their black Wayfarer sunglasses, tucking them away in their inner coat pockets. They walked down the steps, looking every inch like models on the catwalk as flashbulbs exploded. Guests let out a tentative chuckle and a smattering of applause.

Charlotte made her way through the throng to where they were standing. She loved them for showing up. She just loved them, period.

"Gabe!" She ran up to him and gave him a huge, exuberant hug.

"There you are, angel." He smiled as she distributed enthusiastic hugs to the rest of the crew. "I was just about to send the Hoodlums on a search and rescue for you."

"You could have just stood here on the steps. I'm sure I would have noticed sooner or later." She looked at them, laughter fighting with admiration. Laughter won. "Great gams, guys."

"What do you think?" Ryan struck a *Vogue*-like pose. "I'm too sexy for my shorts."

"You guys are too sexy for this party," Charlotte agreed. "What are you doing here?"

The guys didn't say anything, but stared pointedly at Gabe. Gabe cleared his throat. "Well, we discussed it last night, and we thought you might need a little more coaching."

She raised an eyebrow. "Oh, really."

"Well, we were a little...concerned." Gabe looked slightly red, a fact that caused giggles to bubble through her. She never thought she'd see the day that Gabe Donofrio was embarrassed. "I kept thinking about how you said you felt uncomfortable, and how this was going to be awful, and I thought...well, you know."

She took pity on him. "You guys were trying to help, weren't you?"

They nodded, sheepishly. Then devilish grins broke out. "So, how are we doing?" Ryan finally said.

Charlotte couldn't help it. She burst into laughter. It was one of the sweetest, silliest things she'd ever seen. When she finally recovered, she said, "Well, believe it or not, I really am thankful. You're wonderful. Insane, but wonderful."

"And you, hot stuff, are stunning," Mike said, bending over her hand for a courtier-style kiss. Out of the corner of her eye, she noticed Gabe frowning at the action. "So, do you think you'll give me a dance tonight, or are you going to blow me off again?"

"Dance?" Charlotte said. She glanced out at the ballroom floor. Couples were doing a slow sway to an elevator-music version of some popular song. She frowned. "I don't know. This isn't really my style."

"We'll handle that," Gabe said. "Ryan?"

Ryan grinned broadly. "On my way."

She watched Ryan dart over to the leader of the

orchestra. He said his request, then shook the man's hand. She didn't even want to think how much money Ryan was bribing him with.

The song the band was playing limped to a close. Then, after a few moments of silence, the brass section positively exploded into a lively rendition of "Louie, Louie."

The tuxedo- and evening-gown-clad group was stunned yet again. The Hoodlums, however, were in their element. Charlotte didn't know whether to hide or simply laugh as the four men got out there and shook their stuff.

Gabe smiled, taunting her. "Chicken?"

Chicken? Tonight, she could walk on fire. The man had no idea. "Try and keep up with me," she shot back.

With that, she stepped out on the floor and showed them exactly how it was done.

To her surprise, the faces of the crowd were no longer filled with condescension or disdain. They now seemed to be enjoying the spectacle that was livening up what was obviously a traditionally dull party. She noticed several younger couples moving out on the floor and dancing with them. The Hoodlums were a sensation!

The song wound down with a flourish, and Gabe grabbed her and dipped her on the final note. The crowd erupted into applause. There was no laughter, no mocking, just sheer delight.

Gabe picked her up from the dip, ignoring the response of the rest of the audience. "I don't believe it." His smile seemed to be for her alone. "You're incredible, angel."

He had an arm lightly resting around her waist. She was still breathless from dancing. At least, she thought it was from dancing. She put a hand on his chest and could feel his heart pulsing under her hand through his white shirt. His gray eyes shone like beacons.

Without warning, Edna Sheffield stormed over, her face knit in an expression of fury. "Who are you people?"

Gabe and Charlotte jumped away from each other. Charlotte swallowed hard. "Mrs. Sheffield…"

Ryan, Mike and Sean stood in a united front by Gabe. Gabe cleared his throat. "We're the Hoodlums," he said simply, as if that explained everything.

Edna's eyes widened so far that Charlotte was afraid they'd pop right out of their sockets. "The who?"

"No, the Who is a rock band out of England," Ryan corrected her, tongue-in-cheek. "We're a surf crew out of Manhattan Beach."

"A…*surf crew?*" If possible, Edna's eyes widened even farther. "I don't believe this! I'll give you exactly one minute to get…"

"Gabe! It's great you could make it." Jack's smooth baritone floated over as he made his way across the dance floor. He shook Gabe's hand. Charlotte stifled a laugh at Edna's new look of shock. The woman obviously fawned on Jack Landor, proud of his presence at her society function. Now she'd been insulting what looked like his best friend!

"Jack," Gabe said, grinning. "I just thought that the place could use a little livening up."

"Good thinking," Jack said with a laugh, putting a casual arm around Charlotte's shoulders. He smiled down at her. "You looked incredible out there. I didn't know you could dance like that."

She shrugged. "Another one of my party tricks," she said easily. The crew grinned at her. Edna Sheffield remained speechless.

"Hope you don't mind me dancing with your girl," Gabe said in an oddly neutral tone.

"I don't mind who she dances with," Jack said with an easy smile. "After all, I'm the one who's taking her home." He gave Charlotte a quick squeeze. "Which we can do now, by the way. Edna, it's been a wonderful party. Best one in ages, thanks to these guys."

"Ah, thank you, Jack." Edna clearly looked dazed.

"Take care of my friends, will you? I promised this lovely lady I'd have her home early." He glanced down at Charlotte. "Ready?"

She looked at the Hoodlums. All the guys except Gabe were smiling broadly in approval. Gabe just looked off in the distance, a bored expression on his face.

Well, what was she expecting? A pleading look, begging her not to go?

She glanced at Jack. The most eligible bachelor in America wanted to take her home. And tonight, she was capable of anything.

"Home it is," she said, looping her arm through his. "I'll talk to you later, guys."

They whistled at her, making her exit with Jack a very public spectacle. Flashes went off, people applauded.

She resisted sneaking a peek back at the guys as she and Jack finally walked out the door.

Half an hour later, she was still riding the emotional crest that had hit her at the Sheffield Ball when Jack dropped her off at her house.

"I don't know how to thank you, Jack," she said thoughtfully.

He smiled down at her. "For what? You did me the favor, remember?" He nudged her gently. "I've got to say, it's been a long time since I've had a date that great.''

She shook her head. "You don't understand." How could he? For the first time in her life, she felt…beautiful. She didn't care what the other people thought, or said. She felt like a full-blooded *woman*. How could a man understand that a woman never forgot the first time she felt like that?

"All I know is, you were beautiful out there tonight. You were a sensation." He surveyed her for a moment, silent. "So, here we are again. And it's not the first date." He waited expectantly.

Her post-party euphoria fled in a tiny burst of panic. Now what was she going to do?

Wait a minute. She'd been a goddess tonight. She was beautiful, confident and capable of anything. Why shouldn't she try to see if Mr. Right was Jack, after all?

She took a deep breath and closed her eyes.

After a second, he brushed his lips over hers.

She waited.

And felt nothing.

When it stopped, she opened her eyes. "So. That's it, huh?" she asked in all seriousness.

He laughed. "If you've got to ask, then I'm not doing it right." He dipped his face down to hers again. This time, the pressure was a little more insistent, but it was still more friendly than passionate.

All right, this just wasn't *fair*. She was being kissed by a man who was cute, charming, eligible and apparently interested. And her heart rate barely bobbled!

He pulled away, then studied her face with a nod. "How 'bout that time? Anything?"

She sighed. "Maybe I'm undergoing sensory overload," she ventured in a conciliatory tone. "It's been a long night."

"And an eventful one." He shrugged, giving her a lopsided smile that warmed her heart. "All right, pretty girl, I'm off. I'll call you this week if you want to do something."

"Okay." Did she want to see him this week? She had fun with him, but this was getting a little weird. She waved to him as he turned and walked to his gate.

She walked up to her front door pensively. She didn't know what had happened, and that was part of the problem. She didn't really have a lot of experience with men in the physical arena, but she was pretty sure that what had just happened wasn't a good indicator. Good grief. Dead car batteries had more spark than they'd managed to generate!

She was just shutting the door behind her when she heard a rush of footsteps on the walkway. Praying it wasn't Jack again, she cautiously opened the door a crack.

Gabe gave her a breathless smile that gleamed in the moonlight. "Good," he huffed. "You're still up."

"What are you doing here?" she asked, bewildered.

"Um…" He paused for a moment, a blank look on his face. "Would you believe I'm here to pick up the jacket I loaned you yesterday?"

She quirked an eyebrow at him. "If it's the best you could come up with."

"Then that's what I'm here for."

"Come on in," she said, opening the door for him. "I could use somebody to talk to."

He walked in and sat down, groaning with relief. He surveyed her from head to toe, and sent her a warm but tired smile. "That's a pretty cool dress."

She felt a little pulse of warmth shoot through her. "Thanks. I like it."

"You knocked 'em dead tonight."

"And I have you and the Hoodlums to thank for it," she said. She giggled, remembering the look on Edna Sheffield's face. "So, did you decide you'd just had enough of the party, or did Edna go ahead and kick you out?"

"I'd had enough. The guys are still there," Gabe added, grinning. "And Edna tried to hire us as entertainment for her Christmas Gala." He laughed, tucking his tie into his jacket pocket as he undid the top button of his shirt. He took a deep breath. "God, I hate ties."

"I have no sympathy for you," she scoffed, reaching awkwardly for the zipper on the back of her dress. After the disappointing episode with Jack, she could feel the energy of the evening sap out of her. "This whole outfit is like a tie from your neck to your knees, pal. Not to mention the contraption I have to wear underneath. I feel like I need a team of scientists to get it on and off."

"Looks good, though."

She wriggled uncomfortably, her sudden weariness making her fingers fumble. "Do me a favor and unzip me, will you?"

She turned in front of him and waited.

She thought for a moment he must've fallen asleep on the couch. It seemed to take him forever to get up. Finally, he stood behind her. His breath warmed her nape, and she felt an odd shiver in her stomach.

"How'd you get into this?" he muttered, struggling with the zipper.

"Dana helped. She's got a degree in this sort of thing," she whispered, then stopped on a quick exhalation. He slowly unzipped the length of her dress. She was sure that the way the tip of his thumb brushed down the smooth skin between her shoulder blades was purely accidental. Still, she felt her heart pulse, then double in speed, heat curling through her.

"That better?" He leaned over her shoulder, studying her face for a second.

She gulped, nodding quickly.

"Need help with anything else?"

She glanced over her shoulder and saw his gaze riveted to the back of her hooked bustier.

"Um, no." She bit her lip, confused by the sudden rush of blood racing through her. "I can manage from here."

She bolted to her bedroom before he could sense the rapid change that occurred in her breathing, in her body. There was no way he could have realized that her neck and back were two of the most sensitive spots on her body. They were erogenous zones in their own right, something that always embarrassed her. He certainly hadn't done it on purpose.

She was confused enough right now. This was no time to indulge in some strange, adolescent crush on her best friend!

She quickly and awkwardly shed her clothes, dumping them in the dry-cleaning hamper. She threw on a large T-shirt and flannel boxers, taking a deep breath before wandering back out.

"So what did you want to talk about?" he asked. He'd grabbed a glass of water and was comfortably settled in.

She sighed, flopping down next to him on the couch. "I'm confused, Gabe."

"Confused about what, angel?"

She put her head back, staring at her white ceiling. "It was a lot simpler before this whole bet thing got started. I really thought I was happy with my life."

"I know that one," Gabe said, groaning. "The next

time I suggest something that dumb, just haul out and hit me one.''

''Well, it hasn't been all bad,'' she said, stretching a little. He put his arm along the back of the couch, and she rested her head on his bicep. ''I mean, for probably the first time in my life, I felt *pretty*, Gabe. You have no idea what that's like. I have a long way to go, but...it was nice.''

''You looked great, Charlotte.'' Gabe's voice was deep and sincere.

''But then I kissed Jack, and it went to hell in a handbasket.'' She sighed again. ''Now I just wish that I was still watching Raider games with the Hoodlums, and wearing my baggy sweatshirts and jeans, and not worrying about finding Mr. Right because I know there's never going to be one.''

Gabe stayed silent.

''But it's too late now,'' she mused thoughtfully. ''It's like I've opened Pandora's box. I don't want to live like I used to, but I don't know what the heck I'm doing. I feel pretty tonight, but I don't want to keep being what somebody else tells me to look like. Derek tried to change me into something I wasn't. How do I know that Dana and Bella are doing the right thing for me?'' She rubbed her eyes. ''I'm tired, and I just don't know anymore.''

Gabe still didn't say anything.

Finally, she looked over at him. ''Are you asleep?''

He was very still, but his gray eyes were wide-open and piercing. ''You kissed Jack?''

She rolled her eyes. ''Yeah. It wasn't a big deal. Let's just say it was a...chemistry experiment.''

His eyes bore into her. He was quiet for a moment, then nodded, as if he'd decided something. ''Are you seeing him tomorrow?''

''No,'' she said, puzzled. ''Why?''

"Because I thought we might hang out tomorrow, but I didn't want to screw up any previous plans."

She punched him in the shoulder. "You're my best friend, Gabe. It's the Hoodlum motto—Friends Come First."

He finally smiled. "Well, isn't tomorrow a designated date day?"

She shrugged. "Apparently Thursdays through Sundays are, according to my scientific dating team."

"Fine." He took a deep breath. "Charlotte Taylor, will you go out on a friend date with me?"

She narrowed her eyes at him. "That's not like a date-date, right?" she said, laughing. "We go Dutch for dinner, there's no small talk and only minimal groping?"

He burst out laughing, then wound down, breathless. "See, it's stuff like that that I've missed. We've been too damn serious since this whole bet started."

"I know." It had bothered her, too.

"How often do we usually see each other in a week, anyway?"

She rubbed her temples, trying to remember life before this dating-or-death life-style. Simpler times! "I don't know. Four times a week, maybe?"

"Exactly. Out to the movies on Tuesday, football on Saturday or Sunday, or Monday night."

"Or all three," she added. "Or you'd drag your laundry here on Thursdays and watch TV."

"My point exactly." He leaned his head back on the sofa. "How often do we see each other now?"

The point struck home. "Okay. The dating thing has gotten a little out of hand."

"Angel, I'm barely seeing you once a week. I feel like you've moved to Tahiti or something." He ran his fingers distractedly through his hair. "I hate to admit it, but I miss you."

She swallowed the lump that was forming in her throat. "Hah. You've probably just got a load of dirty clothes so big, it's impossible to leave your house."

"Well, there's that, too," he said, chuckling. "But I can always buy a washer and dryer. I can't get another friend like you."

She smiled and moved her head to rest on his shoulder. Like a reflex, he curved his arm around her.

"So I figured, if I have to start scheduling dates with my best friend, then that's what I'll do. Whatever it takes to keep our friendship, angel."

"I don't know how Dana's going to feel about this," Charlotte said, snuggling drowsily against his chest. "She knows how bad I am when I'm with you."

"True enough," he said, wiggling his eyebrows. She sent him a sleepy giggle. "But she didn't say she'd pick *who* you were dating, as long as you were dating, right?"

"A date with Gabe," she mused, lulled by his warmth. He rested his chin on the top of her head, and she chuckled. "Hell has frozen over."

She felt his laughter reverberate through his chest, beneath her cheek. She sleepily realized that she was happy. She wanted to stay like this all night, this warmth curling through her, the deep sound of his breathing beneath her, her arms around him.

So invite him to spend the night.

Mmm.

Wait a minute. What was that?

She suddenly shot up, wide-awake, and got to her feet. She was too tired if she could come up with an idea that preposterous. "I'm falling asleep here, Gabe," she said quickly. "Consider it a date. What do you want to do?"

He smiled and stood next to her. Could she actually

feel waves of heat coming off the man? She took a prudent step toward the door, but he followed her.

"There's a Raider game at eleven, which should give you plenty of time to sleep," he said, winking at her. "After that, I don't know. Maybe a video or something."

Now this was more familiar. "Do I get to pick the movie," she teased, "or is it going to be another testosterone fest where we watch two lines of grunting dialogue and two hours of explosions?"

He laughed. "Fine. Be a girl. You can pick the movie, *and* I'll spring for dinner. Pizza okay?"

"You know it's my favorite."

He rubbed the top of her head with his hand, rumpling her hair. "Groping, of course, is optional. I know you can't keep your hands off of me."

She elbowed him in the ribs, gratified by the "oof" he let out. "Get out of here, you bum," she said, trying not to laugh. This was more normal. After all she'd been through in the past three days, it was about time.

Grateful for his caring, she leaned up to kiss him, a quick, typical peck on the cheek. He must have had the same intention, since he was already leaning down toward her face. She just turned a little too fast.

His lips connected to hers like metal to lodestone, unerring, a magnetic connection. Her eyes widened to see his eyes widen, too, with just as much surprise.

Then his eyes closed, and she was lost.

It couldn't have lasted more than a few seconds, but she felt his mouth move, his lips part fractionally. Every nerve ending she had seemed to tingle to life. She didn't mean to, but she felt her body lean forward, her head tilt back.

It was electric.

He must have felt the current jolt through him, because he jerked back, as if shocked from a socket. He blinked twice, then shrugged. "Um, good night, angel."

"G'night." She hurriedly closed the door behind him, locking the dead bolt. She peered through the peephole at his dark silhouette, strolling down her walkway. Then, on shaky legs, she went over to the kitchen and poured herself a tall glass of ice-cold water.

Okay. If that wasn't irony, she didn't know what was.

Legions of hormones had suddenly snapped to attention with one little, insignificant, accidental kiss. With Gabe, no less. How was that for dumb luck?

Well, at least it cleared up one of the more pressing questions of the evening. She knew it wasn't that she was frigid, or that she'd have problems with getting close to a man. If it had been anyone else but Gabe, that kiss would have gone a lot hotter and a lot longer.

But it was *Gabe,* darn it! Where was the justice in that?

Suddenly, an example from work popped into her head. She'd told her toughest client that just because they'd had a bad experience with one designer didn't mean that they'd have bad luck with all designers. It didn't matter how great the concept was: it had to be designed for the client, or it wouldn't work at all.

You have to go with what works for you…not what people tell you to like.

She smiled. In theory, Jack was perfect, Gabe was pointless. Too bad her body thought otherwise.

Suddenly, she blinked.

That's it!

The advice rolled in her head like thunder. *That* had been the problem with all the makeover stuff. When she was younger, she'd been hesitant to go into fashion designing, thinking it too "girly" and obviously out of her realm. So she'd let other people make those design decisions for her, and she'd ended up with stuff other people had told her to like. She had never trusted her own instincts, until the dress tonight. And she had felt spectacular!

She rushed to her design studio, tearing out a huge sketch pad and breaking into her carefully organized tackle box filled with colored pens. She never felt comfortable in pastels, and she didn't like all those fragile, baby-doll designs. If she stuck with what *she* wanted, what could she come up with?

She tore into the paper, drawing hurriedly, all thoughts of Gabe, Jack, the Hoodlums and the girls gone.

It was brilliant, she thought. And it was going to work.

7

GABE WAS VACUUMING his house at ten o'clock Sunday morning.

That was a strange-enough event. Ordinarily, he believed that Sunday mornings were meant for one thing, and one thing only: to sleep in, waking only to take in food or catch a football game. But his eyes had popped open at around six in the morning, and he could not get back to sleep.

Friend or not, he had a ''date'' with Charlotte.

Not that it was a real date. He'd been very cautious about that, he assured himself, vacuuming around his coffee table. It was all part of a carefully laid-out plan. She'd come over, they'd indulge in all their favorite activities, and it would occur to her that she enjoyed her life just the way it used to be. She would remember how happy she was before she changed her look, before she met Jack, and before Gabe had opened his big fat mouth and very nearly ruined his ''perfect life.'' Then she'd give up man-hunting for good, get back into her old clothes, and things would be just the way they used to be.

He sighed, shutting off the vacuum and grabbing a dust rag. If they could ever be just the way they used to be.

Last night had scared the hell out of him. He'd just about swallowed his tongue when he saw her standing there, a vision in red satin. She'd looked seductive and exotic, and he'd felt an involuntary tug of desire shoot through him before he reminded himself yet again of exactly who she was. He'd had to repeat that little reminder over and over for the rest of the night. When he saw her walk off with Jack, he'd been ready to strangle someone. He'd left immediately after, and gotten to her house with the misguided thought of "protecting" her. If Jack were half as hormonally driven as the average man, he'd have tried anything possible to get Charlotte into bed. Gabe knew that he sure would have.

If he were Jack, that is, he quickly amended. He nervously dusted off his bookcase.

He was relieved to find that Jack wasn't in Charlotte's house last night, but his relief turned to alarm when she asked him to unzip her, revealing all that smooth, creamy skin, and that sexy black bustier. He'd had to get himself a glass of water when she'd been in the other room. He'd almost fled then and there, but by then he'd come up with this crazy "date" plan. At this point, he'd be willing to dress in drag if he thought it might get things back the way they used to be.

He put away the vacuum cleaner and got out paper towels and glass cleaner, heading for his balcony doors. The problem was, as good an idea as this was, he wasn't sure if he could go through with it. His body was starting to boss around his mind, and his conscience…well, frankly, his conscience was always about two minutes too late to really be useful.

He wanted Charlotte. That kiss had come out of the blue, just when he had gotten comfortable. It had sucker-punched him, and he couldn't flee the house quickly enough. He had thought maybe Charlotte had looked dazed, but he hadn't stayed still long enough to really tell.

He'd…well, he'd never really considered her as dating material before. When they'd been younger, she was always that tomboy kid who hung around. When he'd come back from college, she was still grieving over that guy, and he'd felt absurdly protective. He was also still raising hell, and instinctively he knew that Charlotte wasn't that type of woman. She had become his best friend because he could talk to her about things that were too deep to be shared with the Hoodlums, too painful to discuss with his family. When his relationships had gone south, she was the first person he called. When he'd been promoted to vice president at Lone Shark, she was there with a bouquet of cookies on lollipop sticks, of all things. She was the closest person to him on the face of the earth.

No way was he screwing that up because his body had temporarily disconnected itself from his brain. Dammit, it would have been so much easier if she'd just stayed safely shrouded in those sweatshirts and jeans!

He put away all his various cleaning supplies. He plumped up the pillows on his sofa with a vengeance, venting some of the frustration he was feeling. Then he sat down, heavily, sinking into the cushions.

Okay. Obviously, this strange attraction was something they both felt. He knew too much about women not to recognize the bemused look in her eyes and the quickening of her pulse. But he knew that was just because she hadn't really been kissed in years. She was a fledgling, just stepping back out into the sensual world. The idea torched his desire even more, imagining what he could teach her. Brutally, he brought himself back to focus.

One, he thought. She doesn't have these strange

feelings about me, obviously, or she would have invited me to stay.

Two, she is new to this sensual stuff. That made her like a baby rattlesnake: twice as dangerous, because she didn't know about control, and didn't know her own power.

Three, he *did* know how to control himself...and he knew just how lethal she could be.

So what was the answer?

The answer, he told himself firmly, was not to touch her, not get close to her, not do anything that might possibly be misconstrued as *anything.*

He knew what he was doing, he thought, feeling better than he had since this whole thing had snowballed so absurdly. No woman on earth had ever tempted him into turning his back on a friendship, especially one this important.

"Gabe?" He heard Charlotte's voice echo up his stairwell.

"Come on up," he said confidently. It was all good. He could handle it. He was back in control.

She stepped in, arms full of bags and two sketch pads. "Gabe, you have no idea what happened!"

He stared at her. "You're right. What happened?"

"I got hit by the enlightenment stick. Right between the eyes." She dropped the sketch pads on his coffee table, opening them up. The drawings he saw were incredible, but it was fashion stuff. As far as he knew, all she'd ever produced were outstanding logos and corporate designs. These sketches had a vitality he'd never seen before in her work, though.

"Wow." He flipped pages. "These are incredible, angel. What exactly happened?"

"I...well, we don't really need to get into the reason why," she said hastily, "but I finally figured out what was wrong with the whole makeover thing. I'd been going by what Derek wanted me to be, or what Dana wanted or what Bella wanted. Once I figured out what *I* wanted, it was a snap!''

She pointed to the sketch pads. ''I don't like bows, or frills, and I absolutely hate pastels,'' she said enthusiastically. ''If I keep it minimal, and comfortable, I can *still* look good!''

He laughed at her vehemence. ''This should be interesting to see.''

''Wait! I can show you!'' She tore into one of the bags she had lugged up his stairs. He watched with amusement as clothes were suddenly strewn across his extraordinarily immaculate living room. ''I dug out the old sewing machine I used in design school, for exhibit pieces and things, and made up a couple of samples.''

He glanced around. There was a surprising amount of clothes spread out there. ''What time did you finally go to bed?'' he asked, picking up what he assumed was a skirt.

''Huh? Oh. I haven't been to bed yet. I just took a shower and changed into this before I left,'' she said brightly. Then, suddenly, she took off her shirt.

''Hey!'' he said, but before he could stop her, her jeans were unbuttoned and unzipped. They were halfway down her hips before he got to her. ''What are you doing?'' he yelped.

She blinked at him. ''I wanted to show you this outfit. I can't believe I of all people am saying this about clothes, but it's *viciously* sexy. You gotta see it.''

''No,'' he said patiently, trying desperately to stop the blood that had rushed uncomfortably between his legs. Seeing her in a plain white bra and matching panties was viciously sexy enough, thanks very much! ''I mean, why don't you change in the bathroom?''

She laughed. "Have you seen how many outfits I brought over? It would take way too long." She kicked off her jeans and grabbed for a small royal-blue number. "Now, where is the top for this?"

She was killing him, he thought, a protest strangling in his throat. Oh, this had been such a very, *very* bad idea.

She shimmied into the skirt and top. "Now. What do you think of this?" She did a slow turn. "You'll have to imagine the heels, of course, and the cloth is some stuff I was using for color studies for a big exhibit piece I was working on. But it gives the idea."

It gave the idea pretty well, he thought. It wasn't too revealing, but it emphasized her legs and gave a good display of her chest. The color made her skin glow, as if she'd been painted by Rembrandt.

"Very…very nice," he stammered.

"Wait! Wait. I've got a better one in here. Where did I put that?" She tore through the bags again, and he prayed for strength. She started to drop the skirt again and peel off the top.

"Okay, why don't we dump all this stuff in the bathroom, Charlotte?" he said, collecting strewn articles of clothing and averting his eyes. This was more than any red-blooded man could take!

"Gabe, you're holding the dress I wanted to show you.…"

"You know, you're not in any frame of mind for a fashion show," he said hurriedly, still not looking at her. *Remain calm. We can talk her out of this.* "I think you're really on the right track with what you've shown me, but you know me. I'm not any real judge of fashion."

"Gabe," she reminded him, "you're the vice president of a sportswear company."

"Oh." She would have to point out the obvious. "I mean women's fashions."

"Don't you have a women's line, too?"

"On *you,* I mean," he said, finally turning around. Then wished he hadn't.

It was more than a quick glimpse of underwear this time. She was standing there, practically tapping her foot with impatience. Her cotton panties were bikinis cut high on her thighs. Her arms were crossed, and one bra strap was hanging down on her shoulder. Her hair was damp and curling in wavy disarray.

She looked brutally hot. Desire hit him like a tidal wave.

"You're humoring me, aren't you?" she said, eyes narrowed.

It took him a second to form a coherent sentence. "No, I'm not."

She brightened. "Good. Then hand me that deep purple dress you've got in your left hand."

"Charlotte, I *really* think you ought to go change in the other room."

"Why?" she said. "You're just my friend, and there's nothing on me you haven't seen before on someone else."

He sat down. She had summed it all up: he was just her friend. Obviously *she* was having no problem drawing that line. If she was okay with it, then why shouldn't he be? He'd seen plenty of gorgeous babes wearing much less than Charlotte had on.

But he'd never had these kind of restraints on himself, either.

He sat on his couch, trying not to squirm, or even breathe, as she slipped in and out of design after design. She really had a flair, one he would not have suspected, he noticed absently. The clothes she had come up with looked comfortable, amazingly simple, yet they made her look absolutely seductive. The colors weren't at all like the things she had bought when the bet started. They were vibrant, deep colors that made her dark hair and bright eyes look even richer.

Not to mention the effect they were having on his peace of mind.

The worst part of her performance, though, was her little quick changes...a flash of toned muscle, a curve of breast being exposed and then covered by a soft hiss of material. He was being drawn on a rack of self-control, and Charlotte had absolutely no concept of what she was doing to him.

Finally, she got through her last sample and slipped back into her jeans and shirt. He felt as if he was bathed in sweat. His heart was beating as if he'd run a marathon.

"So? What did you think?" she asked eagerly.

What did he think? He thought she'd shaved ten years off of his life with that sensual torture, that's what! "I thought it was...very nice."

"Nice?" She frowned at him, her eyes burning into him like laser beams. "'Nice' is getting a thank-you card. I'm looking for sexy. I'm looking for devastating. Come on, Gabe, work with me!"

"Fine," he said, sighing deeply. "You were incredible. You would make a Buddhist monk pant like a dog. If God had made anything better, he'd have kept it for himself. Now are you satisfied?" He knew he sounded testy, but he couldn't help it. She was just throwing salt on a wound here!

He got up and quickly moved to the kitchen, getting out some ice water. He briefly considered dumping it down the front of his jeans, but settled for taking a bracingly cold gulp instead.

She smiled. "Pant like a dog, huh?"

He sighed. "You're too much, angel."

"That's what I wanted to hear." She yawned, deeply, then settled on his couch. "What time does the game start?"

He cautiously sat down on the couch also, sitting at the far end away from her and grabbing the remote. "Let's see…it's on in about half an hour. I'm sure there's some pre-game stuff on, though. Is that okay?"

"Mmm-hmm." She yawned again, her eyes heavy-lidded.

He smiled tenderly. Now that she was fully dressed again, with no makeup, he felt a little more charitable toward her. She was really cute when she was sleepy like this. She didn't look dangerous at all. "You finally ready for bed, angel?"

She nodded, propping her head up with one arm. "I must be. I was so excited about the design stuff that I felt like I could go on forever, you know? And I had to come over here and show you all of my stuff."

"And you were in such a hurry, you had to show me in my living room?" he asked, trying to laugh about it. To his own ears, he sounded strained.

"Well, it seemed stupid to keep going from one room to the other. You know how I am when I hit a creativity burst." She shrugged, settling more deeply into his couch. "Besides, Gabe, when I hit my break-through, you were the first person I thought of. I wanted you to see it before anybody else."

He felt absurdly touched by her admission. "That's…thank you, Charlotte. I'm honored."

"You're my best friend, Gabe," she murmured. "Without you, I couldn't have come this far. I owe this all to you."

"You don't owe anything to me," he said softly,

watching her drift off into sleep. "You did this all yourself."

The words she mumbled might have been a protest, but in moments, she was sound asleep.

He watched the television screen blankly, unable to focus.

You're my best friend, Gabe.

Easy for her to say, he thought, glancing over at her sleeping form. Now, if he could just keep his hands off her, they could keep it that way.

HOURS LATER, GABE woke up in a darkened room. The TV shone with a blank blue screen. Charlie had woken up briefly for the second half of the game and the first half of the movie. During the second half, they had both fallen asleep. He woke up to find that the movie had run its course and had rewound itself. He glanced at the red clock numbers on his VCR: seven o'clock. He'd been asleep for two hours!

He stretched and started to turn over when his hand fell on a soft, curvy body. Illuminated by the eerie blue, Charlotte was sprawled on the couch next to him. He yanked his hand away.

He smiled. He'd done it. He had spent the whole day with her, doing all of their old favorite stuff. Despite the torturous start, he'd managed to keep his hands off of her, all day long.

He'd kissed her once, he'd seen her half-naked, but that was all in the past. They were just going to be friends from now on. It was perfect.

He felt high with the relief coursing through him. Now all he needed to do was take her out for pizza, and cement the deal. From here on, it was going to be clear sailing.

She was easily startled, so he knelt down next to the back of her head. "Wake up, kiddo," he whispered. "There's a Hawaiian pizza with your name on it."

"Mrmph." She shrugged a shoulder, but she didn't turn to face him.

"Come on, come on. If you sleep now, you'll be up at three in the morning." He gave her shoulders a gentle rub. "You'll feel better with some food."

"Oh," she gasped.

His fingers stopped immediately. "Did that hurt?"

She let out a breathy, half-asleep sigh. "No."

"You nut. You shouldn't have been sewing all night." He increased the pressure, smiling at her groans. "Just call me Gunther, the Swedish masseur...."

"Oh," she breathed again, sharper this time, bowing her back slightly to press against his fingers. "Yeah. Like that."

He looked down to see her body starting to writhe a little on the couch. Her long legs stretched, and her back arched like a cat's.

It was turning him on, he noticed, and stopped abruptly. *We've been doing so well. Don't blow it now!*

"Okay, enough fun," he muttered, turning her to face him. "Charlotte? Come on, wake up."

She blinked for a minute, her eyes half-lidded and slumberous. Her full lips curved into a smile for a second, then she sighed.

"Gabe…"

Before he could move, she reached up and looped her arms around his neck. Before he could think, she had tugged his head down to hers.

By the time he figured out what was going on, he wanted to neither move nor think.

It started out gentle, almost tentative, her lips brushing against his with a whispery caress. He could

feel her breathe his name against his lips, and it shot
fire from his stomach to his groin. He was struggling
for control when she gave him a purring growl and
locked more firmly onto his lips.

Whatever control ' he had left disappeared. He
slanted over her mouth, pushing her back into the
pillows. She sighed and he could feel a shivery tremor
rush through her body. He supported his weight on
his arms, half-covering her body with his own. He
could feel her nipples through the thin T-shirt fabric,
rubbing against his chest. He let out a growl as his
tongue swept past her satiny lips.

He heard her inhale sharply before she arched up
to rub against him, her tongue dueling with his. Leaning on one arm, he used the other to stroke down the
length of her side. His fingers skimmed the column
of her neck and she quivered and cried out against
his mouth. His kisses grew more insistent as he gently
stroked down the side of one smooth, firm breast. She
pressed up against him until he was cupping her
firmly. He brushed a fingertip over a taut nipple, and
she arched up, fitting herself to him with a heated
passion that made him gasp.

He wasn't sure how exactly he wound up on top
of her, but he was fitted at the juncture of her thighs
as she twisted beneath him. She wasn't trying to move
him off of her. On the contrary, he could feel her
thighs inching higher on his hips as she molded herself against his hardness.

It was intense, intoxicating. It was out of control.
His heart was beating so strongly, he could hear it
pounding in his ears like a war drum.

Knock! Knock! Knock!

Wait a minute. That wasn't his heart!

"Gabe, man…are you in there?"

He pulled his head away with effort. Both he and

Charlotte went still, staring at the hallway where the knocks were coming from.

"Come on. We know you're home." It sounded like Ryan. "Don't make us break in there!"

The words sent Gabe rolling off of Charlotte and hurriedly getting to his feet. They were both still breathing heavily. "Don't move," he told her, and went downstairs.

He threw open the door. *"What?"*

Ryan, Mike and Sean were standing at his doorstep. "Jeez, man. We just wanted to let you know the surf's up to eight feet. It's perfect out," Ryan said, gesturing toward the beach. "You coming?"

"You nearly pounded my door down to tell me that *the surf was up?*"

"Of course," Mike said, rolling his eyes. "What's wrong with you?"

Ryan studied him for a second, then grinned. "Whoops. I sense bad timing here…if your jeans are any indication."

"Get lost," Gabe growled.

"Really sorry, man," Mike said, quickly backing away. "Really. Do what you've gotta do."

Ryan started laughing, but Sean looked down at Gabe's driveway and looked back at him, eyes narrowed.

"You sure everything's okay, Gabe?" Sean asked quietly.

"It will be when you clowns get out of here."

The three men left and Gabe shut the door, locking it. He went back upstairs.

Charlotte had hurriedly thrown her pell-mell explosion of clothes back into the bags she'd packed them in, and was tucking her sketch pads under her arms. "You know," she said hastily, avoiding his eyes. "I think I'll take a rain check on the pizza."

"Charlotte, about what happened…"

"I'll take the blame for that one," she said, juggling the sketch pads and the bags. "Really. I guess I was just tired, or dreaming, or something."

"It was a California no-fault accident, angel," he said, nudging her chin up to look in her eyes. "Nobody's to blame here."

She still didn't look directly into his eyes. "I need to get home and get some of this stuff in better shape, so I can make real clothes out of them. And I really ought to…um, do some chores. You know. Around the house."

One minute, she's burning him alive, and now all she could think about was tackling household chores?

"Charlotte, are you all right?"

She finally looked at him, and her hazel eyes were dazed. "I didn't mean for…what just happened to happen. You've got to believe that." She took a deep, quavering breath. "I know it was sort of dumb, but we've been friends for so long, you'll be able to overlook it. I know it didn't mean anything."

It didn't mean anything.

Her cheeks reddened. "I'm just really out of practice with this physical stuff," she admitted in a small voice. "Now, with this whole dating thing, and this whole change of attitude…I guess a lot of things are coming up that I didn't expect."

He nodded.

"I'm going to head out, and we'll just pretend that this never happened. Okay?"

"Sure. Okay." That was exactly what he wanted, about both their kisses. Wasn't it?

She sent him a lopsided smile. She got up on tiptoe and looked as if she were about to kiss his cheek, then changed her mind. She walked instead to the front door. He trailed behind her, puzzled.

"See you," she said as he opened the door for her. "I'll give you a call."

He watched her load her car, then drive off.

He shut the door, locked it and went back upstairs. He sat on the couch for a moment.

She'd left. He'd been kissing the daylights out of her, and she'd just…left.

He realized, of course, that he should be happy about what had happened. He'd been telling himself that getting physically involved with Charlotte would mean problems. It would jeopardize their friendship. It would be disastrous. And despite telling himself all of that, he'd let himself get into a passionate clinch with her, anyway, right there on his couch.

And then she'd gotten up, told him to forget anything had ever happened, and *left!*

This had never happened to him before.

Not that his kisses were irresistible. It was…well, okay, yes, his pride was smarting at that one. But the fact that she could obviously write off what had happened as the overfunctioning of long dormant hormones *hurt,* dammit!

He got up, went over to his fridge and pulled out a beer. He popped off the lid and took a long draw.

She was probably right, he reasoned. They were just friends. No more kisses, pretend nothing happened, and he would finally have his wish, right? Things would be just the way they used to be. He wouldn't have to worry about losing her ever again. Just plain old friends. In a weird, roundabout way, his "date" had gone just as he had planned.

He sighed and downed the rest of his beer. Dammit, why didn't that make him feel better?

8

STUPID. STUPID, STUPID, STUPID.

Charlotte stared at the phone in her bedroom, wondering how she was going to explain to Bella that she couldn't come to her housewarming. "Hi, Bella. I can't show up because I know Gabe is going to be there, and I've been avoiding him for a solid week. Why? Because I shut my brain off, I was half-asleep, and I basically attacked him like an Amazon on his own couch," Charlotte tried experimentally, then stuffed her head in her pillow. "I am so *stupid!*"

She hadn't been thinking at all, that night on Gabe's couch. She certainly hadn't gone over there to seduce him. Seduce Gabe, who had women like that blonde in the restaurant practically tap-dancing naked to get his attention? If anything, he would have been amused by any attempt in that direction.

An image of the kiss flashed across her mind. Images like that had haunted her all week. It hit her in the middle of conversations at work, or when she was grocery shopping, or when she was trying to draw. Or at night, before she fell into a fitful, restless sleep.

It was worst at night.

She sighed deeply. She'd run from his house, apologizing, asking him to forget about the whole thing. By this point, he probably had. But she hadn't, and wouldn't. She knew it wasn't what he wanted. It had probably been pleasant, but he wasn't looking for a relationship with her. And she wanted more than just a relationship, she realized numbly.

She was in love with him.

It was something she should have admitted to herself a long time ago. She was in love with her best friend. When she had no confidence in herself, she had thought just friendship would be enough. In fact, there were times when she felt that his friendship was more than she deserved. But now, with her growing self-awareness, it occurred to her that marriage, family, happy-ever-after were real possibilities.

That is, they were possibilities with men in general. But she wanted Gabe in specific, and that was where the problem was.

She sighed, flopping over the edge of the bed. He wouldn't want to be her Mr. Right. He didn't want to be *anybody's* Mr. Right. Why should he? He could date any woman he wanted. Self-admittedly, his life was "perfect." No, he wouldn't want to throw that all away. He'd never be in love with her.

And that's it? Her conscience sounded indignant. *So now what?*

At any other time, she would have settled for her situation. She would have suffered in silence, just staying friends with Gabe. But she had a real chance now. She felt *pretty*, dammit, and confident. Why should *she* have to be the one to simper and sigh, and wait for him to come to his senses? She had options!

She felt galvanized. She grabbed her purse, digging out a slip of paper, and then reached for her phone.

"Hi, Jack?" She smiled, looking at an outfit she had just finished in her closet. "It's Charlotte. I was wondering…do you think you'd like to go to a housewarming party this afternoon?"

Gabe could do whatever he wanted, she thought, as Jack accepted her invitation. She had her own life to live, and she wasn't going to waste it on dreams that couldn't possibly come true.

GABE HAD BEEN SITTING on Bella's couch, trying to get up the energy to socialize. He was in too bleak a mood since the episode with Charlotte to be very good company.

She'd been avoiding him again, and that was bothering him. They'd talked on the phone a couple of times, but she'd been distant, and he hadn't been able to get her to spill what was going on. Obviously, something was upsetting her, but she wouldn't share what.

She should have been here by now, he thought. He had considered missing Bella's housewarming party, but the lure of finally being able to talk to Charlotte face-to-face had convinced him otherwise. He thought she probably felt awful about what had happened between them last Sunday. She had been embarrassed, possibly even ashamed, at her behavior. She'd even admitted how out of practice she was, as if it were some horrible crime. And all he could do was sit on his hands and take it personally!

Well, he'd straighten her out, he thought, brightening. Granted, they couldn't do it again, but there was absolutely nothing wrong with a few kisses between friends. As confused and worked up as he had felt about the whole thing, it was probably nothing compared to what the poor girl had been going through.

Yeah, right. That's why you've been a hermit since this whole bet started.

Shut up, conscience, Gabe warned. *I don't need your input right now.*

He'd just cheer her up, and they'd go on as usual. She was doing much better, and the clothes she'd designed had seemed to really open a new door for her. In fact, he'd considered asking her if she'd sell a few of the designs for their women's collection. If she'd just *talk* to him for longer than five minutes, if he could…

"Charlotte!" Bella went running to the front door, throwing it open and enveloping Charlotte in a huge hug. "Sorry I haven't seen you since the reception, sweetie, but moving into the house has been such a big production. Besides, I knew you were in Dana's capable hands—"

"Hi, Bella," Charlotte interrupted his sister's usual stream of patter firmly. "I'd like you to meet my friend, Jack Landor. Jack, this is Bella Donofrio…that is, Bella Paulson, now that she's married."

"Congratulations." Jack's deep voice emerged from behind her, and Gabe's eyes shot wide-open. "I've heard so much about you. How was Hawaii?"

Jack Landor was here? With Charlotte? What was *that* all about?

"Oh, just beautiful," Bella said, linking her arm through his. "I'm sorry to have been gone so long and missed all the fun. Charlotte and I haven't been able to talk about *you* nearly enough for my liking." She glanced over at Charlotte, a huge grin on her face.

"Well," Jack said, with a matching grin, "I should be around for a while, so hopefully you can remedy the situation."

Bella laughed, leading the couple to the kitchen. "Can I get you a drink…?"

Great, Gabe thought. Apparently, one of them had managed to put last Sunday behind them as if it were nothing…and it wasn't him.

He got up and slowly made his way to the door of the kitchen, hovering just outside it, by the foyer.

"So this is your new house?" he heard Jack say.

"This is home sweet home," his sister replied. "Brad, why don't you give Jack the grand tour? Charlotte's already seen the house, and she and I need to catch up on some girl talk."

Gabe ducked behind the coatrack, waiting for Jack and Brad to disappear down the hallway before resuming his eavesdropping. He knew he shouldn't, but apparently Charlotte wasn't going to tell him what was going on, and as her best friend, he really had a right to know. At least, that was the justification he was planning on using if he got caught.

"Oh, my God! He is *gorgeous!*" Bella said.

Dana's voice chimed in. "Didn't I tell you?"

"Yes, but it's hard to see exactly how gorgeous he is until he's standing right next to you. A perfect blonde, and that smile! You could tan by that smile!"

Gabe rolled his eyes. If Jack had won Bella's gushing vote of approval, the guy was in for some pressure.

"I love his eyes," Dana cooed dreamily. "That dark, deep green. What's your favorite part of him, Charlotte?" Her voice was amused. "Or can't you tell us?"

Before Gabe could get really irate at that comment, Charlotte broke in firmly. "My favorite part of Jack is that he's sweet and doesn't push me into anything. Unlike you two."

That's my girl, Gabe thought, mentally cheering her on. *You tell 'em!*

"Oh, come on, honey," Dana said, brushing her remark aside. "It wasn't like we put a gun to your head and forced you to take that bet with Gabe, you know. You got into it all on your own. But no matter how you got there, Jack's the sweetest, best-looking date you've ever landed. If we're just trying to encourage you, what's the problem?"

Charlotte didn't say anything, and Gabe strained to hear her response, hoping to finally figure out what was going on.

"I just...I don't want to talk about it. I can't talk about it."

Gabe gritted his teeth in frustration.

"Charlotte? What's wrong?" His sister's voice was concerned. "You've gone all white!"

Gabe started to take a step forward. Sick? Was Charlotte...

"No, it's nothing. I haven't been sleeping well," Charlotte said, and the little irritation in her voice comforted him. If there were something wrong with her, medically, she'd have said something. So what was it? "And I sort of skipped breakfast. I haven't been that hungry lately."

"Well, we'll get you some food, first off," Bella said, switching into maternal mode. "You know what it sounds like? It sounds like you're in love."

In love?

Charlotte, in love with that pretty-boy *Jack?*

"Is Gabe here yet?" Charlotte said instead, and Bella laughed.

"Fine. If you want to change the subject, we'll do it." Dana ignored Charlotte's protests. "If I know Gabe, he's probably camped out in Brad's AV room, watching some sporting event. And no, you can't go find him," she said firmly.

"Honestly, Charlotte, what kind of an impression are you going to make on Jack if you're hooting like a loon with that idiot brother of mine?" Bella added.

Gabe sighed. He was having enough problems with Charlotte. Trust his sister and Dana to make problems even worse!

"I wasn't going to watch sports, and Jack likes me just fine," Charlotte said in an absent tone of voice.

"I just wondered if Gabe was here. I haven't talked to him in like a week."

The room fell silent for a second.

"Okay, what's wrong?" Dana's voice crackled with worry.

"What do you mean?"

"If you're not watching sports, and you're not talking to Gabe, it's an instant code red," Dana explained. "What's going on?"

Gabe leaned forward intently.

"You're not eating, you're not sleeping, and you're...wait a minute," Bella said, slowly. "You're not pregnant, are you?"

Gabe knocked over the coatrack. He caught it just before it hit the floor, in time to hear Charlotte's reaction.

"What? No!" she spluttered.

"Are you sure?"

"Unless you can get pregnant by a handshake and a casual good-night kiss, yes, I'm positive."

Gabe began to breathe again. He didn't mean to feel relieved that Charlotte hadn't slept with Jack, but he did; it was like a weight off his chest. He walked into the kitchen feeling a little bit better. "There you are, Charlotte."

The three women fell silent. His sister and Dana had guilty, cat-and-canary looks on their faces, and small grins. Charlotte just glared at him.

"Anything I should know about, ladies?"

"Just girl talk," Charlotte said shortly. "Nothing you'd be interested in."

"Well, maybe we could talk about something else," he said.

"I've got an idea," Bella said, her eyes snapping with challenge. "How about discussing the fact that

Charlotte's a heck of a lot closer to winning that bet than you gave her credit for?''

"Jack is the catch of the century," Dana said, her voice similarly smug.

Gabe's eyes never left Charlotte's. "Why don't you tell me about Jack, Charlotte?" he said, his voice low. "I don't think I realized how close you two really are."

"There's not much to say," Charlotte said, her chin rising a notch. He knew what that meant: Charlotte's stubbornness was leaping to the fore. "I mean, Jack is a spectacular 'catch,' although I find that really insulting for both of us. He likes spending time with me. I like spending time with him. If he wants more than that, well, we'll see. But for the time being, I'm just trying to spend my time with someone I can actually *envision* having a future with." She arched an eyebrow at him, and he felt a disturbing sense of déjà vu. *This is not for you.* "Does that pose a problem for you, Gabe?"

He gritted his teeth. "Of course not," he replied, his tone just as cool. "Why would it?"

"I think I'll go look for Jack," Charlotte said, smiling sweetly. "I wanted to show him the painting I made for you, Bella. If you'll excuse me?" And without another word, she breezed out into the hallway, disappearing toward the stairs.

"Well," Dana crowed, "I guess she told you!"

"She looks fantastic," Bella said, "but it's not just the new outfit, although it looks like forest green is definitely one of her colors. It's the attitude."

"But I love the clothes," Dana said, smiling. "It looks like our little girl is finally becoming a woman!"

"What do you think, Gabe?" Bella said, smiling.

"I think you two need to stop pushing her," Gabe said harshly, and the two women's eyes widened.

"We're not pushing her," Dana protested. "We're just—"

"You're pushing her. You've never been happy with her the way she is, and now she's changing to please you." Gabe frowned. And he was afraid she'd changed for good. "I'm glad she has more self-confidence, who wouldn't be? But she doesn't need you two nudging her into a relationship she's not ready for."

Bella looked stricken, but Dana's eyes snapped. "She can handle a lot more than you think she can."

"She's a lot more fragile than you think she is," he countered, his voice more gentle. "Trust me, I know. I've hurt her enough. So all I'm saying is, go easy on her, will you?"

Bella nodded. "All right. You know I don't want to hurt Charlotte, ever."

"Of course we don't," Dana said, sighing. "Well, all right, Gabe, but I don't think it's because of us pushing this time. She seems very involved with Jack."

"Maybe." He turned and looked for her in the hallway. He'd just see how involved she was with Jack. As her best friend, it was his responsibility. The last thing he wanted to do was see her hurt…by his sister, Dana, Jack, or even herself.

"THIS HAS BEEN GREAT, Charlotte," Jack said, smiling at her. "Thanks for inviting me."

"No problem." Charlotte took a sip of soda. She was glad he was having such a good time. She, herself, would be having a much better time if she knew where Gabe was. He'd been avoiding talking directly with her, probably from what she said in the kitchen. But it was the truth. Why should she hide from that?

She sighed. It was just that she'd look up and find Gabe staring at her before disappearing. Between that, and the images that would not go away of the episode on his couch, her nerves were quickly getting frazzled.

"You've got a really nice group of friends," Jack continued. "They're like a family. They make me miss my own, actually." He sighed. "They can be sort of pushy, but they love you, you know?"

Her eyes widened. "You could tell that after just a couple of hours?"

He laughed. "I was talking about *my* family, Charlotte. They're always pushing me to get married, that kind of thing."

"I know exactly what you mean," she said with feeling.

"One of these days, I think I'm going to up and elope with somebody, just to get them off my back and get on with my life."

"Hear, hear."

"Charlotte," Jack said, his eyes turning more serious, "have you ever—"

"Excuse me."

Charlotte turned to see Gabe hovering right next to her. "Gabe?"

"Hi. Jack, do you mind if I steal Charlotte for a minute? I needed to talk to her about something sort of private."

Charlotte's eyes widened, but Jack just nodded. "Um, sure. Go right ahead."

Charlotte frowned at Gabe. "I'm sure it's nothing that can't wait...."

"Actually, I have to talk to you *right now*." With

that, Gabe tugged at her arm and started pulling her down the hallway.

"I'll be right back," she said to Jack, then turned to Gabe. "What are you doing?" she demanded.

"Saving your butt," Gabe said, his head craning around. "Bella's got this place filled to the rafters with people, and I need to talk to you in private. Where's…here we go. Come on." He opened a door and led her down the cellar stairs.

She sighed, frustrated. "This had better be good, Gabe," she said, glancing around the darkened room. The air was damp and cool, smelling faintly of lemony detergent.

"Did you hear the line that guy was running on you?" Gabe said, pulling the hanging cord of the lightbulb and turning the light on. "You're lucky I pulled you away when I did."

She blinked in disbelief. "Excuse me?"

"You heard me. That guy was about to make his move." Gabe grinned in smug satisfaction. "Little did he know, huh? You wouldn't buy a bunch of sugarcoated lies about marriage and stuff."

"What makes you think he'd be lying?" she said, anger making her voice sharp. "If he *had* been making a move on me, so what? It's about time somebody did!"

"Are you kidding me?" Gabe replied, his own voice tinged with anger. "Oh, that's rich. Here I am protecting you from a complete lech, and all you can do is give me static about it?"

"Protecting me?" She rolled her eyes. "Please! How many times do I have to tell you—I can take care of myself. I am a full-grown, full-fledged woman who is perfectly able of handling a man who has more on his mind than some casual kissing!"

"Really?" Gabe's voice was sarcastic. "Funny. I

seem to remember a certain 'full-fledged woman' getting distinctly flustered when she found herself just kissing a guy on his couch. I seem to remember her exact words were that she had been 'really out of practice with this physical stuff' for some time.'' His gray eyes were hot as gunmetal. "Or did I just imagine that?"

Trust him to bring up that episode to use against her, she thought, anger making her clench her hands into fists. "I *am* out of practice. Jack could be a perfect way to help me get back into the game."

"Like hell," Gabe growled. "Charlotte, no matter what you think, you don't know what you're getting into. You're way over your head. You don't even know this guy!"

"I do, too, know Jack!"

"After, what, two weeks?" Gabe took a step closer to her, his eyes blazing. "So tell me. What's Jack's favorite sport? His favorite movie? His favorite flavor of ice cream?"

Charlotte stepped toe to toe with him. "He's not a sports fanatic like you, but he'll catch the occasional baseball game. His favorite movie is *Spartacus* and his favorite flavor of ice cream is the same as yours. Mint chocolate chip."

Gabe narrowed his eyes. "I don't suppose you could tell me how he is in bed."

Charlotte gaped, her heart jolting painfully. "How dare you!"

"Of course, you can't compare us there." Gabe smiled coldly. "Maybe I can give you a hint, though, of what I prefer. So you'll know if Jack likes what I do."

Before she could move, he laced his hand in her hair and dragged her mouth up to his.

The kiss wasn't like the warm, simmering, sensual

kiss they'd shared on his couch. If that kiss was like a fireplace, this kiss was like a volcano: hot, pulsating and explosive. His lips flowed over hers, molding her mouth to his. She felt his fingers contract at the base of her neck, while his other arm snaked out to wrap around her waist, pressing her intimately to him.

This was wrong. This was out of anger, out of passion, out of control. And yet it felt so right.

With superhuman effort, she pushed herself from him, tearing her mouth from his. Panting for breath, she glared at him. *"Don't you dare!"*

His eyes widened. He was also short of breath, she noticed. The glint was still there in his eyes, but it banked like coals under cold water at her words. There was more steam than fire. He was getting himself back under control.

Charlotte's voice vibrated with the energy rushing through her veins. "Don't you ever, *ever* just grab me and think you can punish me with that kind of thing, just because you've got some macho, testosterone-driven issues. You aren't Tarzan, and I sure as hell am not Jane." She clenched her fists, passions blurring with fury. "When I kiss someone, it's not going to be out of anger, or frustration, or whatever. It's going to be because of desire, pure and simple. When a man kisses me, it's because he wants to kiss me. You got that?"

He drew a ragged breath, his eyes full of remorse. "I got it."

She nodded sharply. "Good."

Without another word, she threw her arms around his neck, lacing her fingers in his hair, and dragged *his* lips down to meet hers.

If she'd thought she could stay in control of the kiss, she was wrong. Vaguely she thought that she was trying to prove a point, but now all she could hang on to was the fact that she needed his lips, his arms. Him.

He stood stiff as marble, probably with shock, before he wrapped his arms around her, his hands clutching at the small of her back. He melted into her, slanting over her mouth hungrily. She parted her lips, wanting more. His tongue traced her lips with fire. She moaned as his tongue swept into her mouth to tangle with hers. Heat speared through her, pulsing like beacons, drawing a median line from her heart to between her legs. She didn't think, couldn't think. She could only desire, and act.

He pushed her against the laundry table, lifting her up to sit on it. She clutched at his shoulders, and her legs parted easily, urging him to stand between them. His hands stroked down her back in long, loving glides. She could feel his fingertips, like trails of flame that only pitched her passion higher.

"Charlotte," he breathed unevenly against her neck, pressing kisses just behind her ear, down her neck, against her collarbone. She arched her back to press her breasts against him. Her legs wrapped around his waist. He pushed forward, and she gasped.

"Gabe," she whispered, guiding him back up to her lips. The kiss was long, drugging, the slow in and out of their tongues reminiscent of the joining they both wanted.

"Gabe? Charlotte? You down here?"

Charlotte gasped, not in pleasure this time, and thought she'd swallowed her tongue. Or possibly Gabe's. The two of them tore themselves away from each other, standing like panting boxers in opposite corners of the room.

Bella peered down curiously. "Are you two all right? What's going on here?"

"We'll be up in a minute," Gabe said. His voice was rough, and his back was to the stairwell.

"Well, when you do, would you bring up a case of root beer?" she said, then shut the door behind her.

Charlotte's eyes glowed at him. "We've got to stop stopping like this."

"Charlotte, this is crazy," he said, reaching for her and kissing her even as the words tumbled out of his mouth. "If Bella comes back, how are you planning on explaining what we're doing?"

"How about, 'Bella, would you mind coming back after we've had sex on your laundry table?'" She laughed, feeling the blush hit her as it occurred to her...that was precisely where they were heading if they didn't slow down. It was followed by a second thought: she didn't care. She kissed him deeply.

He pulled away, backing up until he hit the railing of the stairway. "Charlotte, I can't do this."

She felt his rejection burn her like acid in her chest. "Of course you can't," she said, then blinked when he leaned down and kissed her again.

"It's just really stupid," he said, kissing her neck and causing her breath to catch, "because I know we're just friends, and—" he brushed a deep kiss over her lips "—we both know this isn't going anywhere. Right?"

"Of course," she said, pressing a kiss back. "Whatever you say."

"If we just work together, I'm sure we can forget that any of this ever happened." He held her to him, tilting her head back and feasting on her mouth.

She couldn't answer him right away, because she had to catch her breath. "Of course," she finally said, not even realizing what she'd agreed to.

Just as quickly, he pulled away from her, walking

to the far end of the room. "Okay, all right, I can handle this." He took a deep breath, waited a few minutes, closed his eyes. "Steer clear of me, Charlotte. I know you've got something going on with Jack, and I knew I shouldn't have let this go on so long, but I couldn't help myself. I swear, if you give me a few days...no, give me at least a week. I'll get it all out of my system. Okay?"

"Gabe, what are you talking about?"

"You're my best friend in the world," he said, dropping a quick kiss on her already-swollen lips. "Please, for both our sakes, stay the hell away from me."

With that, he bolted up the stairs as if demons were chasing him.

Fanning her face, Charlotte leaned back against the now-infamous laundry-room table. What had just happened was...well, it was unbelievable!

He wants you.

It wasn't a matter of her not being his type. It wasn't a matter of him seeing her as only a friend. He thought that she wasn't interested in him. He thought that she only saw him as a buddy!

She might have a shot at this, she thought suddenly. If she was in love with Gabe, and she knew that he wanted her, she owed it to herself to see if a relationship would work. It was easy to think about, to worry about. It was harder to just go and do it. Now, the time for analyzing was over.

This wasn't about his feelings, or their friendship. This was about love...and about her finally putting her fear aside, and going after exactly what she wanted.

If she recalled correctly, there was a chapter in *The Guide* about how to seduce a man. She smiled wickedly. Now was her chance to try it out.

9

A FEW DAYS LATER, Gabe felt that he had perhaps overreacted at the housewarming. He sat at his desk in the office. It was dark out, but he'd been getting a lot done. Yes, given a week's distance and perspective, he felt quite sure that he'd blown the whole thing out of proportion.

"Boss?"

Gabe looked up from the proposal he was working on. "Yes, Jake?"

Gabe's young assistant shifted his weight nervously. "It's about these." He held up several sheets of paper.

Gabe frowned. "What about them?"

"These letters don't make any sense, boss." Jake put them down on the desk in front of Gabe's briefcase. "I mean, in one paragraph, you're talking about the risks of potentially dangerous mergers. Then you're saying we should throw caution to the wind and sign up tomorrow. What exactly did you want to say here?"

Gabe stared at the letters as if they were live snakes. "I wrote that?"

"The really strange thing is, I didn't even think we were trying to merge with this company. I thought we just wanted to run a couple of co-op ads with them." Jake cleared his throat. "I usually just proof your letters and send them as is, but this was really weird."

"I...thanks, Jake." Gabe sighed, taking the letters and throwing them on top of one of the piles on his desk. "I don't know where my head is. I'll fix them. What time is it, anyway?" He glanced at his watch with tired eyes. "Eight o'clock? What are you still doing here?"

Jake shrugged. "If you're working, I'm working."

"While I appreciate the dedication, are you nuts?" Gabe laughed, standing up. He felt tension in his lower back, signaling he'd been at his desk for way too long. "Just because your boss is becoming a workaholic doesn't mean you have to be chained to your desk."

"I thought you must be working on something pretty important," Jake argued. "You've been here until nine o'clock every night, and you're coming in at seven in the morning."

"I'm just... I've been taking it easy this quarter, and I'm just playing a little catch-up. It won't be like this for much longer," He gave Jake a stern look. "And I expect you to work normal hours unless I expressly ask otherwise, got it?"

Jake grinned. "Thanks, boss." With no further prompting, he bolted from the office.

Gabe sighed, shutting down his computer. He might as well admit it. He'd done everything he could think of to exorcise the ghost of Charlotte. He ran on the beach, worked out in his home gym until his muscles screamed, did paperwork until his eyes crossed. Anything to get his mind off her. But that didn't protect him from his subconscious mind. The minute his head hit the pillow, he was asleep with her taste on his lips, the sweet scent of her hair in his nose and the silky feel of her flesh under his palms. He'd relived that moment in the laundry room every night...and had gone considerably further with it than they had in reality, as if they'd never been interrupted. What was worse, when he wasn't fighting this overwhelming lust for her, he got blindsided by an even sneakier emotion.

He missed her.

He'd tried not to call her, but something would happen and his fingers would instinctively start to dial her number. He had consciously avoided poker night and all the usual Hoodlum hangouts, afraid that she might be there. So far, he'd shuttled to work or home, stopping only for long surf sessions because he knew that was one place she wouldn't be. Out in the pounding waves for hours, he could almost forget how close he was to losing her.

He had inadvertently started this change, by proposing the stupid, shortsighted, damnable bet. Now that the change had started, he didn't know what was going to happen to her, or to them. And he didn't know how to stop it…but at the same time, he knew he didn't want to live without her.

He had done everything but talk about this face-to-face with her. Maybe if he just sat down with her and discussed it, she would understand and come up with some way to help him fix things and make it all right again. He'd tried being around her and it had turned into the episode in the laundry room. Now, having tried not being around her, he found she was still just as distracting in his mind as she was in the flesh.

Okay, almost as distracting, he thought, a quick flash of her flesh burning his memory.

They had to talk it out. It was the mature, adult, rational thing to do. Taking a deep breath, he picked up the phone and dialed her number.

"Hello?"

"Charlotte," he said, clearing his throat. "It's me. Gabe."

There was a moment's pause on the other end of the line. "I thought you weren't talking to me," she said finally.

"It's not working, Charlotte. I need to see you."

Another pause. Her voice came through husky, seductively so. "Okay. Where and when?"

He glanced at his watch again. "I'm still at the office, but I was headed home to change out of the suit I'm in…we had clients, so I couldn't wear casual. Maybe I could drop by after that?"

"I've got a better idea," she murmured. "Why don't I meet you at your house? Say, in…half an hour?"

He sighed. Half an hour. He could pull himself together in half an hour. "Okay. I'll see you at eight-thirty."

"I'm glad you called, Gabe." He could hear the little smile in her voice. "I missed you."

She hung up and he gently placed the phone back on its cradle. "I missed you, too," he said, half to himself. And if this worked out, please God, he'd never have to miss her again.

CHARLOTTE LOOKED AT the phone for a long minute.

This is it. This is your one shot at finally letting Gabe know how you feel.

She stood up, trembling. Confidence, schmonfidence. What she needed was a miracle.

She whipped out her now-worn copy of *The Guide*. "Be what he isn't expecting," it advised. "Men love a break in routine. They want something different and exciting."

She scanned down farther. "Meet him at the door in…oh, my goodness." She could feel herself blushing, and she was all alone in the room. "I don't know if I could do that."

But what choice did she have? He'd seen her as a tomboy, as a Hoodlum, as one of his closest and oldest friends. He was just beginning to see her as a potential lover. She needed to get him to make the transition…add friend to lover, and you had a relationship that was worth trying.

She took a deep breath and headed for her sewing machine. She now had created enough outfits to have a small line of her own, she thought proudly. She had really enjoyed doing something that at one time she would have considered so frivolous, but now found challenging and expressive.

She picked up her latest "creation." It was simple, elegant and to the point. It was a midnight-blue teddy, laced up the front with satin ribbon. It emphasized everything it needed to and was devastatingly sexy. It would take guts to wear it…but then again, it would take guts to do what she was about to do.

She took another deep breath, desperately trying to stay calm.

Operation Seduction. Or, more appropriately, Mission Impossible.

GABE HAD GOTTEN HOME and changed into more comfortable clothes and was waiting for Charlotte to get there. He wouldn't let her talk first, and he wouldn't get physically close to her. He'd lay out the problem as if presenting a brainstorming session and see what she had to say. If he just kept his hands off her, if he could just stay focused, they might get out of this alive.

He smiled mockingly at himself. Okay, he was exaggerating. But not by much. This thing had driven him crazy, and he was dangerously close to the breaking point. He was torturing himself with images of her—at the sports bar, at the housewarming, on his couch. If she wore one of her simple-yet-sexy designs tonight, he wasn't sure what he'd do…throw a beach towel over her, or just flat-out tackle her and take her on the living room floor.

He glanced at his hallway cupboard. Maybe he should get out a beach towel, just in case. Either way, he was close to snapping.

The doorbell rang and he started slightly. "Get a grip, man," he muttered to himself, and praying for strength, he opened the door.

She was wearing her hair pulled back, and her makeup made her eyes look smoldering, her lips inviting. He quickly moved his gaze elsewhere. Thankfully, she was wearing a thick gray wool car coat…apparently over one of her shorter dresses, since he couldn't see the hemline. She was wearing a set of low pumps. He quickly glanced away from her legs, knowing that staring too long at them would definitely push him toward the taking-her-on-the-living-room-floor scenario. "Come on in," he said nervously. "Can I get you anything?"

"Um, a glass of water," she said. Strangely, she sounded equally nervous. Probably in reaction to him. He'd been a complete basket case lately. It wouldn't be a surprise if she were uncomfortable with it. And there was their previous and new physical history. Yes, the sooner they got this cleared up, the better.

"Do you want me to take your coat?" he asked.

She looked at him with wide eyes, as if he'd suggested they go murder somebody.

"Um, never mind. Actually, that's better. Keep the coat on," he said, his words tumbling out one over the other. "I have a few things I need to say to you, and I need you to just listen and not interrupt me."

She nodded slowly, nibbling delicately at her lower

lip. He tried not to let the sweet little gesture distract him.

"Charlotte, we've…" he started, then stopped. "What I mean to say is…" He took a deep breath. *Okay, Gabe, just dive in!* "We've kissed, Charlotte. A lot."

She stared at him for a moment, then burst out laughing. "Um, I know that. I was there, remember?"

Her laughter helped break the tension. After a moment, he chuckled, too. "I keep forgetting who I'm talking to. Charlotte, we really need to talk about that."

She smiled, tilting her head to the side. "Okay. What exactly do you need to say?"

His brain went blank for a minute. This was it. Make-or-break moment. "I…well, I guess I forgot it was you when I was kissing you."

She flinched.

"That didn't come out right," he said hastily. "Let me try that again. I mean, I knew it was you, but I sort of forgot everything that *you* entailed."

"And what exactly does kissing *me* entail?"

He sighed raggedly. "I…what I'm about to say here is, ever since you've changed what you looked like, I haven't treated you like a friend, and that's where the problem has been. I just kept getting sidetracked by what you looked like, and ignored the fact that you're Charlotte. And since you're Charlotte…well, you know what that means."

"I'm not sure. Why don't you spell it out for me?"

How long was this agony going to continue? "It means that I shouldn't do anything like that with you. You're…special, Charlotte," he explained. "You're very special to me just the way you are."

She sighed. Without another word, she got up and went into his bedroom.

He blinked. Well, that had gone worse than he had expected. He followed her. "Are you okay…?" he asked, then stopped abruptly.

She had tossed the car coat onto the floor and was rummaging through his chest of drawers. What she was wearing…

He stopped breathing.

Oh, mercy.

She was wearing a deep, dark-blue teddy, in some shiny material that made it shimmer like a black-blue pearl. What little there was was cut high on the thigh and low down the front. It had a dark satin ribbon lacing it up the front, just begging to be untied. She turned to stare at him, her eyes huge and glowing like hazel crystals.

"Do you have any sweats?" she asked.

He cleared his throat. "I'm sorry. What?"

"Sweats," she repeated, blushing. The pink wash covered most of her body, it seemed, and he could tell…most of her body was deliciously exposed. "I was wondering if I could borrow a pair of sweats and a T-shirt."

His mouth went dry. He tried to look everywhere, all at once, and his pulse beat a hectic tempo in his chest.

She looked down at the drawer she'd opened. "Look, I feel really stupid about this. I should have known…oh, I've just been an idiot. Sure, I've changed a lot, but we've always been just friends. I guess I was starting to buy the hype, you know? Charlotte the Tomboy turning into Charlotte the Sexy. It's like we always say…you know you're in trouble when you start believing your own press."

He barely registered the self-derision in her voice, the embarrassment. A part of him wanted to comfort her, but the rest of him had already started the chem-

ical change that made listening or even rational
thought impossible.

The beast was awake, and it wanted Charlotte.
Gabe had finally reached his breaking point. He
snapped.

"I just want to throw on some normal clothes and
watch ESPN until I forget this whole episode
ever...hey!" Her words got cut off as in two quick
steps he was at her side, spinning her, grabbing her.
Taking her.

With an impatient motion, he pulled the ribbon out
of her hair, crushing the satiny waves in one hand.
His eyes burned into hers. Before she could say anything else, he molded his mouth to hers, branding her.
She tasted like some tropical fruit, sweet and tart and
exotic. He feasted on her.

When he felt her body melt into pliancy, he gripped
her to him, gently tugging at her hair until her closed
eyes opened. "I tried, dammit," he said, his voice
ragged. "I tried not to do this."

She took a deep breath. "Do you know who I am
this time?"

He nodded. "You're the woman I told myself I
couldn't want, but the woman that I need more than
breathing. You're the woman I crave like a drug."
He smiled, his eyes gleaming with ferocious promise.
"You're the woman I'm going to make lose control
tonight. Satisfied?"

She started to nod. "Well, not yet," she said, and
her voice sent sensual shivers from his heart to his
stomach, and lower. "But I think I will be."

"Charlotte," he groaned, and took her mouth
again.

This was what she wanted, she thought. She returned his kiss with a fierceness she didn't know she
was capable of, tangling her fingers in his dark hair.

She moaned, low in her throat, as her tongue dueled with his.

It was only a few steps to the bed, and she laughed as they stumbled over a pair of his running shoes and tumbled onto it.

He laughed, too, a short, harsh gasp. "Okay, I'm going faster than I should," he said, studying her intently. "I've wanted you for too long to lose control now."

"Be careful," she warned, moving her body seductively and grinning smugly when his eyes widened. "You're not the only person who can make somebody lose control." She kissed him gently on his jawline, then lay back on the bed and smiled.

He raised his eyebrow at her challenge. Then he ran his fingers through her hair, his fingertips caressing her face like a blind man, learning with his touch the way he'd only known her with his eyes. "You are exquisite," he said, his voice low and rough. "Don't ever doubt it." He brushed kisses over the trail his fingers had drawn.

He made her feel beautiful. Her fingers went to his shirt. The trembling of her hands made her go much more slowly than she wanted to, but the sensation of material drawn slowly over his now-sensitized skin was having an effect on him. Finally, she tugged the thing off his shoulders and tossed it blindly onto the floor.

She took a minute to look her fill at his broad, muscular chest. Then she skimmed her fingertips over it, taking her cue from him, moving with gentle roughness. The satin smoothness of his skin contrasted wildly with the corded muscles that flexed under her hands.

He smiled that sexy, devilish smile that sent a spear

of fire through her chest. "My turn," he murmured against the base of her throat.

She gasped at the sensation, feeling ripples of it pulse through her chest. He took the ends of the ribbon that laced up her teddy and slowly tugged. The bow vanished. Then he eased the shoulder straps down off her shoulders. "This is nice," he said appreciatively, grinning. "I think you should greet me at the door in this more often."

"Well, you know how it is," she teased, breathlessly. "Laundry day's tomorrow, and it's all I had left...."

He laughed, tracing the low edge of the now-open bodice with his tongue. "Remind me to bring a load of laundry over," he said, his breath tickling her skin. "I think I'd like to know you're not wearing anything when I get there."

She was going to chuckle, but he edged the material lower and she didn't have any more breath to laugh with.

She was amazing. He cupped the undersides of her breasts and teased her through the satiny material. He watched as her nipples grew rock hard under his attention, and smiled tenderly as she edged up to meet his mouth. She was breathing in sexy little gasps, a combination of surprise and arousal. She moved like a dancer, all grace and strength. She pulled her head up and kissed him, nipping at his throat with sharp little teeth. It threatened to send him over the edge, to just grip her and take her.

The glint of sexual challenge in her eyes only encouraged him to take it even more slowly, to torture her the way she was torturing him. He'd take all night and part of the morning if he had to.

He slipped the teddy off her, and revised that thought. He'd last maybe five minutes at this rate.

Her body was perfection. Firm, high breasts over a toned stomach, hips flaring out into curvaceous legs. She twisted a little, obviously unused to being naked to the light of a man's eyes. The little action made him smile.

He stroked her legs lovingly, promising himself that he'd give more attention to them later, when he wasn't under the driving, brutal passion that was grilling him as he caressed her.

She grasped one of his hands. "No fair," she said breathlessly. "It's your turn." She reached for his waistband. He gave her a surprised look. For someone so shy, she took the lead with a look of hunger that tripled what he was already feeling. If this kept up, he might die. But he would certainly die happy.

She was struggling for control as he lay back on the bed, grinning, encouraging her. She undid the button and zipper on his jeans, then eased them off.

He was wearing silk boxers with a dark paisley pattern. She could see the evidence of his arousal springing forward against the slick fabric. She tossed the jeans aside, then paused. "Aren't those the boxers I bought you for your birthday?"

He started to nod, then hissed sharply as she smoothed her hands over them, giving loving attention to his hardness. "Mmm. They didn't feel this good in the box."

He choked.

She laughed, teasing him the way he'd teased her, pressing kisses on his legs, on his chest, at his waistband. Before she could dip lower, he growled, pinning her on the bed. "You keep that up, angel, and I'll be embarrassed. I want tonight to be good for you."

"Gabe," she whispered, pausing to kiss him deeply. "I'm finally with you. It's already perfect."

He smiled, like a man who'd been given the gift he'd always dreamed of, and she shivered as he took her mouth in a kiss sweeter than any she'd ever experienced.

The sweetness converted to hunger, and hunger to fire. She'd always been self-conscious about her body, the first to dive under the covers in her long-ago romantic episodes. She'd never felt particularly confident in bed, for that matter. But tonight was different. Tonight she felt like all those women she'd only read about…temptresses, seductresses. Women men went crazy for. Women men loved.

When he leaned down to kiss her neck, she moaned, wrapping her arms around him, stroking strong, eager fingers down his back. He nipped at her breasts, making her trembling even more pronounced.

"Gabe," she said, clutching at him. "Please. I need…"

He groaned. "Angel, I need you, too."

He tugged off his boxers.

He was magnificent. His skin was gleaming and chiseled. He reminded her of a Donatello bronze that she'd studied in school. Except that his arousal was…

She cleared her throat nervously. *He's huge.*

Something must have reflected in her face, because despite the passion that was clearly burning through him, Gabe chuckled. "Second thoughts, angel?"

"Eep."

He laughed, nuzzling at her neck. She could feel the pounding in his chest, echoing the reckless pulse in hers. He kissed her throat, stroking her back with butterfly-light touches that had her melting into him like butter on toast. When she felt his hardness pressing at the soft flesh of her thighs, a wave of molten dampness answered between her legs. She arched her hips up, cuddling him intimately.

He stopped, poised at the brink of her. His breathing was labored. "Charlotte."

She looked up. His eyes were rings of blazing silver around circles of opaque black fire.

"You'd better want me as much as I want you, because from here on there's no stopping."

It took her a minute to figure out what he was saying, drenched in passion as she was. He was giving her one last chance to stop what they'd started. He was letting her decide.

The fever inside her was beyond reasoning. She arched up against him, kissing him fiercely as she moved her legs to curve around him.

With a groan, he pressed forward, and she felt him fill her with delicious slowness. She gasped, loud. "Gabe..."

"Oh God, angel," he breathed.

He moved inside her, rocking with gentle thoroughness. She could feel the pressure of him, moving over her most delicate flesh, and felt fire roar through her. She pushed her hips up to meet him, wrapping her legs tightly around his.

"Gabe," she breathed. "I can't...I'm..." Her pulse pounded in her ears and she was shouting his name.

He moved against her, and she could feel the slick sweat between them. He was bringing her to the edge, and she could feel that elusive pulse start to ring through her. She pushed against him, and he drove into her, hard.

She was catapulted over into oblivion, every sense overloading. She cried out, clenching him tight. *"Gabe!"*

"Charlotte," he groaned in answer, and his hips jerked hard against hers, once, twice.

He sunk on top of her, their arms twined around

each other, as if they could never let go. After a long moment, he pushed himself up on one arm, stroking her sweat-dampened bangs out of her face. He smiled rakishly.

"I won," he said.

She blinked. "You won what?"

"I made you lose control first." He leaned onto his back, carrying her with him until she was sprawled on top of him. He kissed her quickly. "So, do I get anything? Fabulous cash prizes? A trip to Bermuda?"

She chuckled. Her head was still reeling from what they'd just done. And amazingly, as his fingers stroked down between her shoulder blades, she felt an aftershock of pleasure. She squirmed and his eyes widened as she rubbed against him.

"I think you were cheating," she said, moving seductively, her breathing going shallow. *This is ridiculous. You just had a sexual experience that nearly blinded you! And you're ready to do it* again?

His breathing went uneven, but he smiled. "What are you suggesting?"

She leaned down and kissed him luxuriously, until they were both breathless and gasping. "Tiebreaker," she said, when she could finally speak.

"Two out of three?" he said, moving up with one lusciously rough motion.

She gasped. "You're on."

10

GABE WOKE UP SLOWLY, sensing the sunlight pouring in through his window. He was hot, was the first thing that came to mind. And a little cramped, now that he thought about it. But strangely, he wasn't uncomfortable. In fact, he had an overwhelming feeling of well being, bordering on satiation. Hell, he felt happy. And when was the last time he'd faced a morning with *that* emotion?

He started to roll over and encountered a girl-shaped lump.

He froze.

It was his apartment, his bed. His best friend.

Oh, no.

He had just made love with Charlotte. Several times, in fact.

The shock of what he'd done was nothing compared to the jolt he got as he remembered the night before. He'd told himself, he'd *promised* himself that he wouldn't touch her. He'd just talk it out and be adult about the whole thing! He'd explain what was happening, and then he'd be able to keep his best friend, instead of getting into bed with her, which would lead to a relationship that would be doomed to failure. He *knew* what was at stake and still he had been the stereotypical guy, letting his body do all the talking!

If he had known this was going to happen, he

would have locked himself in, unplugged his phone and sat in his living room with the lights out.

He closed his eyes as more images of the previous night invaded. Or would he?

He tried to calm the unruly response of his body, which even now reacted to the memories of what they'd done. He'd never kissed a woman the way he'd kissed Charlotte. Those kisses weren't a maneuver to get her to sleep with him. He'd kissed her that way because he needed her, because she felt so perfectly right beneath him. And once she'd gotten there, the whole thing had changed. She'd turned into... Well, he couldn't quite describe *what* she'd turned into.

All he could say was, they'd gone five out of seven, and she'd won. And he never would have expected that his best friend Charlotte Taylor would be his perfect sexual complement in bed.

She was sexier than he'd ever dreamed anyone could be, her body like silk and fire. That generous mouth of hers, moving over him...

Now he leaped out of bed. Okay, no more thoughts down that path, or he'd be sure to get into more trouble than he was already in!

He couldn't resist looking at her, though, and the sight made his heart beat unevenly. She was tangled in the sheets, still completely naked. Her body looked lean and graceful. Her hair was tousled and her face was relaxed, her full lips still curving in the remnants of a smile. She had a mark on her neck where he'd kissed her a little harder than he realized.

He leaned down, pressing his lips gently where the mark was. She gave a soft little sigh, turning toward him blindly.

He pulled back as if burned.

He hastily snatched up some clothes and dove into the bathroom. Putting himself under the spray of the shower, he berated himself. Charlotte wasn't a Saturday night pickup or the Babe of the Week. She was, quite possibly, the most important woman he'd ever met. He couldn't use her like this.

Maybe you weren't using her.

The thought was quiet, sneaky, and he growled under his breath. Ah, the ever-helpful conscience. He was wondering when that would show up. And, as usual, it provided no helpful advice whatsoever. He didn't want a relationship with anyone, much less the one woman he knew he needed to keep by him for the rest of his life. If he got into a relationship with her, he'd lose her, it was as simple as that. Honestly, what was his conscience thinking?

Okay, that's it. I'm letting you screw this one up all by yourself.

It's about time, Gabe thought as he got out of the shower and hastily toweled himself off. Then he caught a glimpse of himself in the foggy mirror. His eyes were wild, and he was frowning and muttering.

He was in worse shape than he thought. He was actually arguing with himself!

He got dressed and walked through the bedroom. Charlotte was still sleeping, obviously exhausted. When he saw her, he didn't see what he had in every other relationship. He knew that he'd never ride an emotional roller coaster with her. He wouldn't see jealousy, he wouldn't be forced into little dramas and psychological showdowns. She wouldn't ever hurt him.

As long as she was his *friend.*

But he knew her. She was looking to get married, to be wildly in love. She *deserved* to be in love, even though his chest ached uncomfortably at the thought. She didn't deserve to be hurt because her best friend was an ass. If she had been any other woman, he'd have convinced her to call in sick and they would have spent the day in bed, finding new and exciting ways to enjoy each other. Then, once he'd figured out what it was he couldn't stand, or once she'd played one too many games or thrown one too many tantrums or just gotten a little too clingy, he'd gently break it off and go back to his old life.

He knew there was no way he would feel, or do, any of that to Charlotte. At least, he wouldn't do it intentionally. But what if it did happen? She wouldn't bring in expectations, but she would leave with disappointments. There was no way he could keep her as the friend he needed. And he needed her desperately. God, how he needed her.

Damage control, he thought. *Stop this now, before it gets worse.*

He grabbed a piece of paper and a pen. "Charlotte," he wrote. "Meet me at Hennessy's at seven-thirty. Gabe."

Sighing, he left it on the bedside table. Then, because he couldn't help himself, he lowered his head and kissed her. Even asleep, she stirred beneath his lips, pressing against him. He let himself linger for just a second. *After she sees me tonight, I'll never be able to touch her again.*

He tore himself away.

Got to stop this now, he told himself, locking the door behind him. *Before it's too late.*

"WHAT IS *WITH* you today?" Wanda snapped.

Charlotte stopped, midstride, a dazed smile on her face. "Huh? What are you talking about?"

"You're singing." Wanda's finely drawn eyebrow lifted. "You never sing."

Ryan walked up to her. "You've been dancing in the hallway, too. What's going on, girl?"

"Nothing. I'm happy." Charlotte hugged her folder of sketches to her chest. "Did somebody pass a happiness law when I wasn't looking or something?"

"You're more than happy," Wanda said with some asperity, studying her as if she were a bug under a microscope. "You're glowing."

Ryan squinted, then stopped, his eyes widening. "Oh, no."

Charlotte mistrusted that expression on his face. "What?"

"You got lucky, didn't you?" Ryan crowed with laughter. "Wait till Gabe gets a load of this!"

Charlotte winced.

Wanda snapped her fingers. "That's it! I thought I recognized that look!" She pursed her lips. "I've just never seen it on Charlotte before, that's all."

"Meeeow." Ryan glanced at Wanda, grinning. "Sheathe those claws, Catwoman. So, Charlotte, who's the lucky guy?"

"Remind me again how this became your business," Charlotte retorted, making a beeline toward her office. Ryan and Wanda were hot on her heels.

"Aw, come on, Charlotte. How can you expect me to leave a prime piece of gossip like this one alone? The rest of the Hoodlums have a right to know!"

"Yeah, Charlotte," Wanda said, practically purring. "You can't keep this a secret."

"Right to know? Freedom to gossip is not covered in the constitution!" Charlotte tried to be more angry about it, but the fact was, she was too ecstatic to even care that they were hassling her. "My sex life is private, as in none-of-your-business private. Only one other person is privy to the details." She smirked, winking at Ryan. "And that's only because it wouldn't be any fun if he *didn't* know, you know?"

Ryan roared with laughter as Wanda gaped. "At least tell me this," Ryan hounded. "How was it?"

"How was it?" Hard as she tried, her pulse picked up and she felt the dumb grin she'd been wearing all day broaden. "It was incredible. Out of this world." She stopped, seeing them at the edge of their figurative seats, drinking in every word. "It was just fine, thank you very much. Now, if you'll excuse me, I've got work to do." *Way to be discreet, Charlotte!*

She began to close the door, but Wanda grabbed the door handle. Her green eyes widened. "Oooh! You have a hickey!"

Charlotte's hand flew to her throat, where the makeup she'd so carefully applied must have worn off.

"Charlotte's got a hick-ey, Charlotte's got a hick-ey!" Ryan sang cheerfully.

"Grow up," she groaned, before slamming the door in their faces. She could hear the chanting and hooting laughter for another minute or so before Ryan finally disappeared, his chuckles echoing down the hallway.

She sat down, putting her folder on her desk. She was going to get no work done today, she could tell that right now. Anything she drew would have hearts and flowers on it...or be very, very risqué.

Last night had been more than incredible. She didn't have words to describe the experience. Anything she might have expected was completely surpassed.

And best of all, she'd won, she thought with a wicked grin.

She shook her head, feeling her pulse increase as the heat built in the pit of her stomach. Oh, she wanted him. It had been creeping up on her all morning, no matter what she was doing or who she was talking to. She could not get Gabe out of her mind.

How was she supposed to know that her best friend for twenty years was the man of her dreams?

But he was more than just her best friend now. The image of him would be irrevocably linked to an image of the two of them, tangled in sheets and each other. She would never be able to look at him and just think "weekend football" or "poker night." How could they just share a couch without thinking of what had happened when they'd finally shared a bed?

Not to say that they weren't still friends. To her mind, that's what made it all so perfect. She knew his heart, his secret dreams and fears. He knew hers. There wasn't any awkward getting-to-know-you period, no hesitancy. There was nothing they couldn't share with each other. They clicked so perfectly before; now they were meshed. They were one heart.

She'd always known that she loved him, as a friend. Now she valued his friendship as a lover.

He hadn't woken her up this morning, which was just as well. She would have pounced on him again and neither of them would have made it in to work. She'd never felt that way about Derek, this insatiable hunger. Of course, one man could hardly be considered a control group. If she'd met someone like Gabe to start with, maybe she would have had the hunger sooner.

If I had started with Gabe, I never would have moved on to anybody else.

She glanced down at the note he had left by her bedside. Meet him at Hennessy's. She smiled. Funny that he should pick one of the Hoodlums' hangouts. Maybe he wanted to make their new status public as soon as possible. She'd only been to Hennessy's a few times herself. It was more of a guy's place, a real pickup joint. She seemed to remember they had some nickname for it, but she couldn't recall it offhand. It probably involved "babe-hunting," if she knew the guys.

She smiled, hugging herself as she felt goose bumps crawl up her arms. Gabe wouldn't have to look very far to find a "babe" tonight, she decided. Tonight was the first night of her new future. She shook her hair out of its ponytail, letting it fall in loose waves over her shoulders.

Last night she'd been a goddess, fiery and unconquerable. It had been Gabe's tenderness and passion, and her own confidence, that had finally gotten her there. She couldn't go back to what she was. She didn't want to. Tonight, she was going to show Gabe exactly how sexy he made her feel.

She grinned. And she was going to show him until the sun came up tomorrow morning.

GABE SAT AT ONE of the high, round tables at Hennessy's. It was the height of happy hour, with plenty of men and women laughing, flirting and generally being rowdy as they munched on the buffet and ordered rounds of margaritas. He nursed his beer, glancing at his watch. She would be there any minute. The rest of the Hoodlums called Hennessy's "Heartbreak Hotel," because at one point or another, they had all brought women there to break up with them. It was a perfect setting for it—public, loud, hard to cause a scene in. He had picked it out of habit, and out of cowardice. He wasn't sure how Charlotte was going to handle the news that last night had been a mistake, a poor decision that their overexcited bodies had thrown them into. For that matter, he wasn't sure how he was handling it himself.

He'd rather put a gun to his head than hurt Charlotte. He knew that. But this was the only way to prevent her from getting even more hurt later. He had a chance to catch it now, quickly, before it went too far.

Of course, you're assuming that last night meant as much to her as it did to you.

Ah, my conscience, he thought. He'd been beginning to miss it.

He took a long draw of his beer. Of course it meant as much to her. No one could have gone through what they went through and not have felt the power of it. Just memories of their night together sent pulses of heat through him. He'd been with more women than he cared to remember, but he had never had as intense an experience as he'd had with Charlotte.

But it had to be more than just an experience, dammit. She deserved more. He rubbed his hands wearily over his face. Why in the hell had he slept with her? She was his little Charlie, his best friend, his pal. The tomboy. The one who could play poker or football, help you fix your car or hear you out. She was the perfect sidekick. She wasn't the type of woman you fell in love with, right?

He looked up, midthought, and his breath caught in his throat.

She was standing in the doorway, looking as if she'd just stepped off the Babe of the Week Web site…or better yet, off some runway in Milan. She had on a little black dress with those teeny shoulder straps that made his eyes pop. The dress had a slick, satiny sheen that seemed to take what little light there was in the place and caress it over her curves. It clung to her body like a lover. Her hair was up in a simple twist, framing her face like a work of art. Her eyes looked huge, like hazel-green gems. She looked like a painting, or a sculpture. Or a goddess. She wore deep, dark lipstick, emphasizing the quirk of a smile, and showing just how immensely kissable that mobile mouth of hers was.

He tore his gaze away. *Oh, my God.*

As he glanced away from her, he noticed that he wasn't the only man who'd been struck by Charlotte's entrance. He noted the predatory interest showing on the faces of several of the men around him. It was all he could do not to beat the gleam of lechery off of their smug, beer-guzzling faces. She spotted him, waved to him, her smile growing sexier by degrees. She started walking. She was wearing high heels and her hips swayed hypnotically as she strode toward him.

"Hi, Charlotte," he said hoarsely, leaning forward to be heard over the noisy din of the crowd.

"Hi," she said huskily, then moved in to kiss him.

The urge to kiss back was strong, but he dodged. Her kiss landed on his cheek. She gave him a puzzled glance, looking around. "What? Are the guys here or something?"

He wiped the lipstick off his face. "No. At least, I haven't seen them."

She smiled, sending heat straight to his groin. "I thought about you all day. Thanks for letting me sleep in, by the way." The smile grew more intense. "If you hadn't, I don't think we would have made it in to work today."

Hearing his cowardice interpreted as thoughtfulness, and hearing his own thought from that morning come from her sexy lips, sent pangs of pain through him. He took a deep breath. "Charlotte, we need to talk."

She went still. She reminded him of a nature documentary he'd seen of a gazelle scenting a lion. Her eyes were wary. "Do we?" she asked, reaching over and taking a sip of his beer.

He nodded, taking a deep, aching breath. "It's about last night."

She nodded slowly in return. "What about last night?"

"Last night was…incredible." He hadn't meant to say that, but it was the truth. She deserved to hear it.

Her eyes lit with sultry fire. "Tell me about it."

"But it was probably not a great idea." He saw her eyes widen, and he plunged forward, as if saying the words faster would somehow lessen the blow. "You're my best friend, angel. I don't want to do anything to hurt you, but we've known each other way too long for me to lie to you. You want somebody to fall head over heels in love with you. You want to get married. You deserve that." He swallowed hard. "You deserve better than some fling with me."

She blinked. He felt like he'd slapped her.

"Angel?" Gabe finally said, after a long, pregnant pause. He reached out for her hand, but she didn't take it. He sighed. "Come on. Talk to me. We can always talk to each other, right?"

She continued studying him, shaking her head. Without a word, she began to tremble, putting her head down on the table into her cradled arms.

She was crying. Oh, God, he was such scum. He reached over to stroke her silken, soft hair. "Oh, Charlotte, I'm so sorry…."

Her head popped up, and she wiped at the tears at the corners of her eyes. And that's when it hit him.

She was laughing.

"Oh, for pity's sake, Gabe. You are *such* an idiot," she announced, taking a deep, hitching breath between laughs.

"I beg your pardon?"

"As well you should," she said, between chuckles. "Could you be a little more into yourself?"

Now he felt like *she'd* slapped *him.* Reeling from the shock, he finally stammered, "What are you talking about, Charlotte?"

"Have you taken a good look at me lately?" She stood up, did a slow twirl that caught the eye of every man in the bar. She leaned forward so only he could hear her. "For the first time in my life, I feel *beautiful.* Desirable. It's been a slow, uphill process, but now that I've got it…sweetie, there's no way a rejection from you is going to ruin all that."

He watched the way her eyes shone, and his hand reached out to stroke her cheek before he could stop himself. "Of course not. I never thought that it would."

She pulled away, her eyes flashing. "What I'm trying to tell you is that I'm a big girl now, Gabe. I'm not little Charlotte whom you need to protect. If you feel you can't handle a relationship with me, that's fine. But don't you dare think you can pin this on 'protecting' me, because that just won't cut it."

"But I wasn't—" he started, then cut himself off. Well, in a way, he *was* trying to protect her. He was trying to protect them both. And what was wrong with that?

"We can agree on one thing, though. I'm glad you said something before this went any further. Neither of us needs the drama."

"Well, I'm glad you're not hurt," he said numbly. Funny that his own chest felt like a glacier, tearing a cold path through his heart.

"Are we done with this, then?" She picked up her purse in a businesslike fashion. "I've got to get going."

"Why? Got a date?" He regretted the question as soon as it was out of his mouth.

She surveyed him wryly. "No offense, Gabe, but I've got this whole life *besides* you, you know. And amazing as it sounds, it appears that I *do* have a good chance of getting married and having a wonderful husband and family. In a way, it's all thanks to you." She leaned over and brushed a quick kiss on his cheek. "I'll let you pay me that thousand in installments. Got to run. I'll catch you later."

"When?"

She shrugged. "I don't know. My social life just got a lot more hectic. I'll call you."

She turned to go.

"Charlotte?"

She turned, sighing. "Yes?"

He swallowed hard. "You know I love you, right?"

Did he see the pain shoot across her face, or did he just imagine it? Her face was now a mask of amused tolerance. She shrugged. "Of course I know that, Gabe. But you're not *in* love with me, and I guess we both know that." She sighed. "Maybe we just need a little breathing room. This is all getting too crazy. Steer clear of me for a while."

He watched as she walked slowly across the floor, smiling at various men as she made her way to the door. One man stopped her. Gabe was on his feet before he realized he'd moved.

She simply smiled, patted the man on his shoulder while shaking her head and laughing at something the man said. Then she walked out, every male gaze riveted to her. With her head held high and her hips swaying gently, Gabe could only think of two things.

She was so beautiful, his heart ached to look at her.

She was walking out of his life forever.

11
———————

"CHARLOTTE, HONEY, can we talk?"

Charlotte glanced over at Dana, barely hearing her over the pounding beat of the dance club. "Something wrong?"

Dana turned to where Bella, Brad, Jack, and Dana's husband, Stan, were sitting off to the side. She motioned to Bella, who nodded and hurried over to join them. Charlotte frowned when the two women tugged her outside. The night air was refreshingly cool, and she bloused out the top of her dress.

"Charlotte, we're worried about you," Dana said, in her usual straightforward manner.

"Worried about me?" Charlotte knew from the look of concern etched on both of their faces that this conversation was going to be a doozy. "Why? I'm fine."

"You are *not* fine," Bella contradicted her gently.

"I really appreciate you going out with me as much as you have in the past week, but the truth is, I haven't had a social life this jam-packed since…" Charlotte thought about it. "Actually, I've never had a social life like this." She adjusted the fit of the short cherry-red dress she was wearing. "I've had men stop me on the street and ask me for my phone number. I've been hit on at the grocery store. Somebody tried to pick me up at a stoplight, for pity's sake. It's the most bizarre thing I've ever seen." And it was. Any other time, she would be bewildered by the attention, possibly even frightened by it. But after what happened with Gabe, it didn't matter in the slightest. Very little did. If anything, she was somewhat amused.

"Yes, your social life is skyrocketing," Dana admitted. "But that's not excessive dating that's putting those shadows in your eyes. And have you lost a little weight?"

"Upped my workout a little bit," Charlotte explained, not adding that she'd needed to wear herself out to get a few hours of sleep at night. "And I suppose I've been running myself a little ragged, between work and all of this going out. I'll rest more this weekend, I promise."

"Charlotte," Bella said gently, "nobody could be more pleased than we are that you've blossomed so beautifully. What's more, that you believe in yourself." She crossed her arms. "But we know that you're not happy. Not really."

Charlotte replied impatiently. "First, I'm not paying enough attention to my appearance, and you say you'd leave me alone if you thought I was happy. Now I'm painting the town red and you say you'd leave me alone if you thought I was happy. There's just no pleasing some people!"

Dana and Bella could have been twins, the look of concern and caring on their faces was so similar. They stared at her, waiting for her to speak, ignoring her waspish remark. They also obviously weren't going anywhere until they found out what was wrong.

Charlotte sighed. She loved them for loving her, for trying so hard to help her. But she needed to do this on her own.

"Let me tell you a little story," Charlotte finally said, her voice calm and detached. "Say you take a woman who doesn't have much confidence in her looks, who hides behind being a tomboy. Say you add a man who is kind and loving with a perfect sense of humor. Someone who she could easily spend the rest of her life with.'' She felt her voice catching in her throat, and she focused on the wall of the club, rather than Dana's and Bella's sympathetic eyes. ''That man shows her that not only is she beautiful, she's exquisite and extraordinary. He brings things out of her that she's never felt with anyone else. Say that woman decides she's completely, madly in love and spends the night with him, expecting it to be the beginning of happily ever after.'' She glanced at them. ''Only instead of a relationship, he decides at that point that they would be better off as friends.''

Dana gasped in outrage, while Bella simply nodded sadly, encouraging her to go on.

''The woman now has two choices. She can do what she's always done before…retreat behind her baggy clothes and straggly hair, and never let a man suspect what she's really like. Never let any man hurt her, ever again.'' Charlotte sent them a watery smile. ''Or she can remember one very important thing that the man taught her: he may have shown her how special she was, but he didn't *make* her special. She's special all on her own. And if he can't appreciate that, that's his problem. Not hers.''

''Oh, honey.'' With that, the two women threw their arms around her in a big, comforting hug.

''So maybe I'm not happy,'' Charlotte whispered. ''But for the first time in a long time, I can honestly say that I'm fine.''

They stood there like that for a minute, drawing strength from one another, giving strength to one another. After a minute, they stepped apart, each mopping at her eyes.

"Charlotte, I'm so proud of you," Dana said, wiping at a small blot of mascara. "If I were you, I'd be egging his car right now."

Charlotte laughed. "Well, it had crossed my mind."

Bella looked resolved. "I'm going to tell Gabe that the stupid bet is off. You don't need one more hassle hanging over your head, when you've obviously got so much more important things going on!"

"The bet has been the last thing on my mind. I think Gabe's pretty much decided to forget it, too." Charlotte was glad her voice stayed steady. Even saying his name was difficult.

"Well, I'm so mad I could spit," Dana said, her green eyes flashing with fire. "Who does that guy think he is, anyway? Mr. Most Eligible Bachelor in America! I tell you, if I had him in front of me, I'd make sure his next photo shoot looked like a police report!"

Charlotte stared at her. "What are you talking about?"

Bella sighed. "She's just mad at Jack, Charlotte. We'd have to be blind not to put it together."

Oh, God. Charlotte shook her head quickly. "It wasn't Jack."

Now both women stared at her. "It wasn't?" Dana asked. "Then who was it?"

"I'm not telling you." Charlotte's chin jutted up, determined. "This is my problem, and I'll handle it on my own."

Dana looked ready to argue, but Bella put a hand on her shoulder. "Looks like our little girl has grown up," Bella murmured, smiling.

Charlotte gave each of them a hug. "That, and I don't want you to egg his car."

"WHOO-EE. THE BABES are out tonight!" Ryan said, handing a beer to Mike.

Mike grinned, eyeing the crowd. "Honey alert, twelve o'clock. Get a look at that one, Gabe!"

Gabe swirled his soda around in his glass. He gave the woman a cursory glance, then shrugged.

Mike huffed, nudging Sean. "What is *up* with this man lately?"

Sean studied Gabe intently. "Offhand, I'd say woman trouble."

Ryan gave Gabe a quick glance, then laughed. "No question. Only a woman, or lack thereof, could make a guy this miserable."

"Now that you mention it, he hasn't gotten a lot of action lately. Maybe you should try diving back into the dating pool, bud," Mike suggested helpfully. "This is a target-rich environment. I'm sure there are a ton of babes here who'd love to be your flavor of the month."

"Hah. Of the weekend, maybe, knowing our man's track record," Ryan corrected him.

Gabe ignored them, letting their voices blend into the din. He stared at the tabletop, sighing.

He could remember the past week in crystal-clear detail. His life was a steady routine. He worked out. He surfed. His job was going like clockwork, and he was getting a lot done. Some of what he'd come up with was even usable. He was also going out with the guys every night, something he hadn't done in years. His life was going fine, just fine.

Sure he missed Charlotte. She was his best friend, why shouldn't he miss her? So he'd reached for the phone to call her a couple of times a day. Big deal. And he'd canceled poker night. She was one of the best poker players there. It was pointless to keep playing without that level of competition.

He'd given the football games last Saturday and Sunday a miss, too. There was such a thing as too much football, even for a guy like him. Just because he couldn't watch it with Charlotte didn't mean anything.

"Hello?" Sean nudged Gabe sharply in the ribs. "Check out the redhead coming this way."

Gabe glanced up halfheartedly. A voluptuous woman with flame-red hair was slinking her way to their table, a knowing smile on her pouty lips. The Hoodlums smiled broadly.

She walked straight to Gabe. "Hi there. My name's Melissande."

He nodded.

She smiled, and he felt her chest brush across his shoulder. "You don't seem to be having a good time here. Is there any place I could take you, and maybe help you feel better?"

He could sense the barely concealed glee from the other men at the table. He shook his head. "No. Thanks."

Her eyes widened in obvious surprise. She leaned over a little farther. "Are you sure? I'm very, very good…at cheering people up."

He turned to her, shrugging her touch off of his shoulder. "I don't mean to be rude about this, but I'm not interested. Okay?"

He turned back to his beer, hearing rather than seeing her flounce of indignation.

The guys watched her walk away, then pounced on him. "Are you out of your mind? That woman was hot!"

He glared at them. They ignored his obvious attempt to shut them up.

"Maybe it's Charlotte," Ryan said suddenly.

Gabe's head jerked up. "What the hell are you talking about?"

Ryan shrugged. "Well, the fact that she's finally gotten lucky has got to mean that you're that much closer to losing your bet. But I wouldn't worry too much about it. I mean, she's dating like crazy, but I thinks it's still impossible for her to get somebody to marry her in a week, man."

"How do you know she's 'gotten lucky'?" Gabe asked in a low, chilling voice.

"She had a hickey the size of Cleveland under her jaw, that's how." Ryan laughed. "Happened a week ago."

Mike gasped. "Charlie? Our Charlie?"

"Our Charlie has got to be a lot happier than our cheerful friend here, is all I can say," Ryan said sagely. "Maybe you should take a page out of her book, man, and lighten up. The day after she got that monster, she was so lit up you could have used her for a scoreboard."

"Is she still happy? Shown any more...marks?" Gabe asked, more sharply than he'd intended. Had she found someone that quickly? *That was what you said she deserved,* his conscience asserted. His chest obviously disagreed. The dull ache intensified at the thought of someone else enjoying her luscious body, her bright, sweet smile. Her.

Mike turned to Ryan curiously, but Sean continued to stare at Gabe, his eyes narrowing. Gabe was too intent on Ryan's answer to care.

Ryan frowned. "Now that you mention it, I don't think so. I mean, she's working a lot, but she seems to go out with a different guy every night, and out to lunch with another one every day. While I'll say she's a lot more, er, social than she's ever been, no way is our Charlie easy." On that point he looked adamant.

"So what happened to the guy who gave her the hickey?" Gabe prodded. "She's never mentioned who it is?"

"Well, no," Ryan admitted, shrugging. "But it's pretty obvious, don't you think?"

Gabe held his breath.

"It's gotta be Jack. He was the only guy she was dating around that time that I know of."

"Well, whoever it was, he's one lucky man," Mike said, chortling. "I may have to give her a call, myself...."

Gabe reached across the table and went for Mike's throat.

"Hey!" The other men quickly disengaged Gabe's hands from their friend's neck. "What are you doing, man?"

"Don't talk that way about Charlotte," Gabe demanded, his hands shaking in rage. "Not when I'm around. Not around anybody. If I find out you've said anything about her to anyone, I'll tear you apart."

"I wasn't disrespecting Charlotte, Gabe!" Mike yelled, rubbing at his neck. "What the hell is *wrong* with you?"

Ryan shook his head. "Oh, no."

Gabe turned to face him, ready to take him on, too. "What's *your* problem?"

"I should have realized. You're being sullen, irrational, touchy and hair-trigger violent." Ryan sighed indulgently. "Why didn't you tell us you're in love, man? We could have packed up all your breakables."

"I am *not* in love," Gabe growled. And that was the one thing he could be thankful for. Like he didn't have enough problems right now! "Being in love makes a man crazy. It always ends in disaster, and it's always with the wrong woman. I'm not doing any of that!''

He stormed away, but not before hearing the Hoodlums say in unison, ''Yup. He's in love.''

JACK DROPPED CHARLOTTE OFF at her house that night. She was glad to see him, but she felt a slight awkwardness after everything that had happened between her and Gabe. Still, Jack had been understanding about her other dates. He'd been downright wonderful about keeping her busy, too. He took her to movies, out to dinner, even on a trip to the zoo once. But she could sense a growing tension from him, a sort of uneasiness that intensified every time she saw him. Whatever it was, it was getting worse, she surmised. He hadn't said anything to her the whole car ride back, and that was unlike him.

He walked her to her door, as usual. ''I guess this is good night, Jack,'' she said, giving him a quick hug. She hadn't kissed him since that disastrous smooch after the Black and White Ball. This time, he kept his arms around her loosely. ''What is it?'' she finally asked.

''This is sort of rough for me to talk about,'' Jack said haltingly. ''Have I ever told you about my family?''

''No,'' she said, with some surprise. ''Now that you mention it, you've always listened to me, but you haven't told me much about yourself.''

''They're wonderful, don't get me wrong,'' he began, but his eyes looked troubled. ''My father is a publisher, you've probably read that much. He and my mother are the greatest, but they've really been pushing me lately. Between them and the press hounding me, I feel like I've been unable to get anything important accomplished, and I've given up meeting anybody who will just care about me for me. I'm at the end of my rope. It's like no one will leave me alone, you know?''

Charlotte smiled. ''Actually, I do know. Dana and Bella have been like that for years. You don't want to be pushed around by them, but you love them, and you don't know how to say no.''

''That's it. That's it exactly.''

She sighed. ''I've finally gotten them to calm down somewhat, but now and then, I wonder if I shouldn't just change my name, shave my head and run away to join the circus.''

He smiled sadly. ''I've got an easier solution, sort of,'' he muttered, sighing heavily. ''But it's crazy.''

''Jack, we're friends,'' Charlotte said, and meant it. ''You can tell me. What's wrong?''

''You're going to think I'm insane, but I was just wondering...would you do me a favor?''

He looked so at a loss, her heart immediately went out to him. ''Anything for a friend, Jack. What is it?''

''Do you think you could marry me for a while?''

12

"WHERE'S CHARLOTTE?" Mike looked around expectantly. "I thought she said she'd play today. It's the Hoodlum Super Bowl."

"We're sort of...not talking right now." Gabe shrugged, trying to remain cool and ignore the pain the words brought. "But she's fine, don't worry about it."

"Who's worried?" Mike frowned, then laughed as realization dawned on him. "Oh, I get it. You pissed her off again, didn't you? What'd you do this time?"

I lost her. "I didn't do anything."

Sean gave him a quizzical look. "Maybe that's what pissed her off."

Gabe leveled a steely glare at him. "Shut up and throw the damn ball, okay?"

The other guys playing immediately started catcalling and taunting him before settling down to play some serious football. Half an hour later, their jeers had been replaced with groans of pain.

"Dammit, Gabe," Mike muttered, rubbing at his ribs. "This is touch football, man, not the NFL. Go easy, will you?"

Sean grabbed Gabe roughly by his collar. "Time out!" he called to the others, dragging Gabe toward the crashing surf. When they were out of earshot, Sean let him have it. "What is up with you, Gabe?

You almost killed Mike, but you haven't caught a single pass I've thrown to you. Where is your *head?*''

Gabe shook off Sean's grip with a rough shrug. ''I don't know.''

''It's the girl, isn't it?'' Sean gave him a rough pat. ''What's she into now?''

''It's not so much what she's into. It's what I'm into. Or not into. What I…that is…'' Gabe growled in frustration. ''I slept with her.''

Sean simply looked at him, nodding. ''Like that's somehow a shock.''

Gabe blinked at him. Didn't he understand? ''I said, I *slept* with her.''

''So? Charlotte's beautiful,'' Sean said, smiling wistfully. ''I've entertained some daydreams myself. But she's, like, your soul mate. I mean, the guys are close and all, but that woman knows your heart. So you did something about it.'' Sean shrugged. ''So what's the problem?''

Gabe stood, silent.

''I mean, you told her you loved her, right?''

Still nothing.

''You *do* love her, right?'' Sean emphasized his words, as if talking to a child. ''I'll kick your ass if you think you don't, because nobody disrespects our girl that way. Least of all an idiot who can't see the truth when it's staring him in the face.''

''I don't know what I was thinking,'' Gabe rasped. ''All I know is, I made that stupid bet, and suddenly nothing was the same. She was still Charlotte, sure, but she was wearing those clothes, and we were spending all this time together, like we always do…and then something changed. I did everything I could think of to get us just to be friends again,'' he argued, "but it just happened. I couldn't stop my-self."

Sean sighed. "I sense stupidity ahead. What did you do after that?"

"I stopped it before it got worse," Gabe said, closing his eyes. The incident still played through his head every night. If he wasn't thinking of the night they'd spent together, that is. "I thought maybe I could catch it in time, that I wouldn't screw up the friendship completely, but I was too late. Now she won't see me or talk to me. I don't know what to do." He opened his eyes, looking over at Sean. "It was just what I thought would happen. I don't know what I'm going to do without her."

"Gabe, you're like a brother to me, right? So I'm going to tell you this from the heart." Sean put a heavy hand on his shoulder. "You're a schmuck."

Gabe blinked. "Sorry?"

"You heard me. You're in love, man."

Gabe thought about it for a minute. "I don't believe this," he said slowly, even as the truth began to hit him. "Even if I am…that's not going to help me. I can't make a relationship work. I never have."

"Those other women you thought you were in love with. That was bull. You weren't in love with them. Heavily in lust, addicted to drama, but not in love."

"I tried to make them work," Gabe said. "They all just fell apart, no matter what I did. That's when I made the rule—friends over commitments."

"And do you know why?" Sean's dark eyes bore into Gabe. "Because *you always had Charlotte.* She was always the first person you called when one of the women you believed you were 'in love with' went haywire. If you had a problem, or good news, or if she needed you, then you two were together, no mat-

ter who you were dating. They had your body, but
Charlotte's always had your heart.''

Gabe stopped, started to speak, then stopped again.

''This time, you've got a shot at the whole thing—
marriage, kids, the whole nine yards. And you're
scared.'' Sean shook his head. ''Scared of all that, but
even more, scared of screwing up the most important
thing in your life and losing her. So what did you
do?''

Gabe sighed. ''I screwed up and lost her.''

''Bingo. So what do you think all this means?''

Gabe stood for a minute, staring at the waves.
He never wanted to see Charlotte with another
man. He couldn't stand all the time he'd spent without
her. He needed her smile, her laughter, and most of
all, her love.

''It means I'm in love with Charlotte, and I'm going to do something about it.''

''All this time together, and you're just figuring it
out.'' Sean sighed. ''It's things like this that convince
women we're idiots, man.''

Suddenly, Ryan came running down the beach,
crowing and waving a newspaper.

''Ryan, don't you wear a watch?'' Mike yelled as
Ryan approached the group. ''You're two hours
late!''

''You've gotta see this,'' Ryan answered, puffing
from his run. The guys crowded around him, and he
pushed a tabloid into Gabe's hands.

''What the...'' Gabe gaze fell on a full-color picture of Charlotte and Jack in a tabloid. The lurid head-
line jumped out at him: Lady in Red to Wed Jack
Landor?

''Isn't it a scream?'' Ryan's face broke into a wide,

foolish grin. "Our honorary girl Hoodlum, getting married to the Most Eligible Bachelor in America?"

Gabe watched, detached, as his fingers twisted the paper, practically ripping it in two. He barely heard Ryan's yelp of protest.

"You've got to go, Gabe." Gabe looked up, and Sean's face was solemn. "It's not too late."

Gabe made a break for his car, praying Sean was right.

CHARLOTTE WAS EATING LUNCH outside at Martha's Café with Dana and Bella. She wasn't looking forward to her conversation with them, but it had to be done. They would notice when she suddenly, after a few weeks of mad socializing, stopped dating anyone at all and disappeared from the scene.

What she really wasn't looking forward to was explaining *why*.

"So I finally told him, I don't care whose wedding you're working on, you promised me two hundred orchids for tonight's banquet and I don't want to hear another word about it." Dana nodded sharply, and Bella laughed. "Honestly! Like I'm going to let him put me on the hot seat at work because some Arabian prince needs centerpieces!" She glanced over at Charlotte, winked. "Now, if it were Jack Landor's wedding, that would be something else...."

Before Charlotte could question that, Bella sent her a piercing, inquisitive look. "Speaking of, is there anything you'd like to tell us?"

"Well, yes..." Charlotte said, then frowned as the tone of her question sunk in. "Wait a minute. What are *you* talking about?"

"Charlotte, it's been in all the tabloids," Dana said in a rush. "There's a picture of you in that red dress, and there are all these rumors that you're going to get married!''

"We wanted to wait until you told us," Bella said with a brilliant smile. "But you were taking so long, we just couldn't hold out! So what happened? How did he propose to you?"

"And when's the wedding?" Dana asked, jumping in. "I'm so excited, I could pop! Imagine, just like you thought, a proposal in under a month!"

"Now, hold it just a second," Charlotte said firmly. "Jack did propose, but I need to explain a few things...."

"Charlotte."

She stopped, midsentence. Taking a deep breath, she turned. "Hello, Gabe," she said quietly. Her fingers tensed on her glass of lemonade.

"Ooh, Gabe, have you heard?" Dana's voice was bright and, to her credit, only a little smug. "He proposed! Jack proposed to her!"

"So the papers claim. I thought I'd find out for myself what the story was." His voice was low and dangerously husky. "It took me a little while to track you down, but I need to talk to you, Charlotte."

He looked like hell, Charlotte thought, her heart aching. He had a rough day's growth of beard, and his hair was windblown and careless. It would have made him look more rugged, like Indiana Jones, if it weren't for the shadows in his eyes. He looked like a man fighting demons.

Every fiber in her being wanted to stand up and throw herself into his arms. But she just sat there. "Couldn't believe it, huh?"

"I didn't want to, but yes, I believed it." His eyes gleamed silver and lightning. "I just wanted to hear the truth from you."

She struggled to keep her voice calm. "If you must know, yes, Jack did propose to me."

"I see," he said, his voice low.

She barely noticed the excited sounds from Dana and Bella. It was as if the world had narrowed to encompass just herself and Gabe.

With a slow, deliberate motion, Gabe reached into his leather jacket pocket and pulled out his check-book. "I guess you win, angel. As it happens, I have the check right here."

Dana and Bella high-fived.

Charlotte's heart broke, splintering like glass. She showed no outward signs. Her face remained impassive and her eyes were glued to the check in his out-stretched hand.

"It's yours," he said. "Just come here and get it."

Like a marionette, she got up and walked to where he was standing. On the front of the check, in his bold handwriting, was the amount: one thousand dollars. And written in a scrawl on the memo line was a small sentence.

"'Congratulations to the winner'?" she read aloud.

He nodded.

She would rip it up and throw it in his face, she thought. Then she'd leave and never see him again.

She reached for the check.

With a quick motion, he grabbed her wrist, pulling her to him, molding her to him. She looked into his tortured eyes just before his mouth dipped down to hers and she felt the inferno that built whenever they kissed.

"Double or nothing," he whispered against her lips. "I bet you that I can make you happier in the next fifty years than that guy could have ever made you. I swear."

She felt a wild surge of happiness but pulled back a little, tugging against the hands that caressed her back and looped her in his embrace. "Gabe…"

"Yes?" His voice was tender yet rough.

"Are you saying this because you love me," she asked carefully, "or are you just a sore loser?"

His eyes widened in shock, just before a chuckle emerged, growing into the rich laughter that she loved so much. "Okay, I deserved that one. But let me explain." He pulled back enough to look into her eyes, his gray gaze level and sincere. "I didn't know that this was what being in love was. I always thought that love was this big production, with all the drama and screaming, and everything that went with it. But then I figured out that I was just scared. Scared of screwing up and losing the most important woman in my life. So what did I do? I went ahead and did just what I was most scared of."

"You know, this is why women think men are idiots," she teased.

"What? Am I wearing a sign?" He laughed softly, nuzzling her neck, then turned serious. "Even when I thought I was in love, I never shared myself with those women the way I did with you. Nobody knows me like you do." He stroked her cheek, his smile like the sun. "And nobody matches me as perfectly as you do. I love you, and I'm in love with you. Say you'll marry me, Charlotte."

"I told Jack I was too in love with you to marry anybody else. There wouldn't be anybody else I'd marry," she said vehemently. She leaned forward and shared a passionate kiss with him, relishing the feeling of his arms tight around her, as if he'd never let go again.

"Um, excuse me?"

Gabe and Charlotte turned and looked over at the lunch tables. Women all over the café were misty-eyed, and several were sighing deeply. Bella looked as if she were in shock. Dana, on the other hand, simply looked flabbergasted.

"Would somebody like to explain what's going on here?" she asked.

Charlotte looked up at Gabe and smiled. "We decided to make another bet. And this time, we'll both win."

Modern Romance™
...seduction and
passion guaranteed

Tender Romance™
...love affairs that
last a lifetime

Sensual Romance™
...sassy, sexy and
seductive

Blaze™
...sultry days and
steamy nights

Medical Romance™
...medical drama on
the pulse

Historical Romance™
...rich, vivid and
passionate

27 new titles every month.

*With all kinds of Romance for
every kind of mood...*

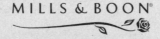

MILLS & BOON®

Modern Romance™

THE BLACKMAILED BRIDE *by Kim Lawrence*

A classic romantic fantasy with a colourful, upbeat mood! Kate was determined to protect her sister from scandal – and Javier Montero was the only man who could help. But Javier wanted something in return. As head of his family's business empire, he needed a wife. Kate was about to become a blackmailed bride!

THE SICILIAN'S WIFE *by Kate Walker*

Enjoy the sizzling sexual tension and a proud Sicilian hero! Marriage to Cesare Santorino is all Megan has ever wanted – but not like this! She's in deep trouble and has no choice but to agree to a mutually beneficial, convenient union. Cesare makes no secret of his passion for her, but Megan hopes that he'll come to see her as more than just the body that he desires…

THE DOCTOR'S SECRET CHILD *by Catherine Spencer*

Experience deep emotion in this tale of young lovers reunited… When Molly Paget fell pregnant, her father made her leave town. Nobody knew about the baby – including Molly's ex-lover Dan Cordell. Now a family crisis sees Molly's return as a successful businesswoman with a young daughter. But what happens when doctor Dan learns about their child?

THE MARRIAGE DEBT *by Daphne Clair*

An intensely passionate read! Shannon's new project offers international success. But she needs millions of dollars in funding and the only person she knows with that kind of money is her estranged husband, Devin Keynes. Devin agrees to help on one condition: she gives their marriage another chance…

On sale 5th July 2002

Available at most branches of WH Smith, Tesco, Martins, Borders, Eason, Sainsbury's and most good paperback bookshops.

0602/01b

FREE
2 BOOKS
AND A SURPRISE GIFT!

We would like to take this opportunity to thank you for reading this Mills & Boon® book by offering you the chance to take TWO more specially selected titles from the Modern Romance™ series absolutely FREE! We're also making this offer to introduce you to the benefits of the Reader Service™ —

★ FREE home delivery
★ FREE monthly Newsletter
★ FREE gifts and competitions
★ Exclusive Reader Service discount
★ Books available before they're in the shops

Accepting these FREE books and gift places you under no obligation to buy; you may cancel at any time, even after receiving your free shipment. Simply complete your details below and return the entire page to the address below. *You don't even need a stamp!*

YES! Please send me 2 free Modern Romance™ books and a surprise gift. I understand that unless you hear from me, I will receive 4 superb new titles every month for just £2.55 each, postage and packing free. I am under no obligation to purchase any books and may cancel my subscription at any time. The free books and gift will be mine to keep in any case.

P2ZEC

Ms/Mrs/Miss/Mr ....Initials ....
BLOCK CAPITALS PLEASE

Surname ....

Address ....

....

....Postcode ....

Send this whole page to:
UK: FREEPOST CN81, Croydon, CR9 3WZ.
EIRE: PO Box 4546, Kilcock, County Kildare (stamp required)